**love yo**
**library**
**ND**

**Buckingh** **RSON** is one of the best-known and
**S ... ch. re** writers of all time. His books have sold in
excess of 350 million copies worldwide. He is the author of
some of the most popular series of the past two decades –
the Alex Cross, Women's Murder Club, Detective Michael
Bennett and Private novels – and he has written many other
number one bestsellers including romance novels and stand-
alone thrillers.

James is passionate about encouraging children to read.
Inspired by his own son who was a reluctant reader, he also
writes a range of books for young readers including the
Middle School, I Funny, Treasure Hunters, House of Robots,
Confessions and Maximum Ride series. James has donated
millions in grants to independent bookshops and he has
been the most borrowed author in UK libraries for the past
ten years in a row. He lives in Florida with his wife and son.

# BOOK**SHOTS**

## STORIES AT THE SPEED OF LIFE

What you are holding in your hands right now is no ordinary book, it's a BookShot.

BookShots are page-turning stories by James Patterson and other writers that can be read in one sitting.

Each and every one is fast-paced, 100% story-driven; a shot of pure entertainment guaranteed to satisfy.

Available as new, compact paperbacks, ebooks and audio, everywhere books are sold.

BookShots – the ultimate form of storytelling. From the ultimate storyteller.

# AFTER THE END

## JAMES PATTERSON

### WITH BRENDAN DuBOIS

BOOK**SHOTS**

1 3 5 7 9 10 8 6 4 2

BookShots
20 Vauxhall Bridge Road
London SW1V 2SA

BookShots is part of the Penguin Random House group of companies
whose addresses can be found at global.penguinrandomhouse.com

Penguin
Random House
UK

First published by BookShots in 2017

www.penguin.co.uk

A CIP catalogue record for this book is available from the British Library

ISBN 9781786531940

Typeset in Garamond Premier Pro font 11/15.5 pt by Jouve (UK), Milton Keynes
Printed and bound in Great Britain by Clays Ltd, St Ives Plc

MIX
Paper from
responsible sources
FSC® C018179

Penguin Random House is committed to a sustainable future
for our business, our readers and our planet. This book is made
from Forest Stewardship Council® certified paper.

# AFTER
# THE
# END

# CHAPTER 1

**IT'S A GORGEOUS** day along the frozen shores of Lake Marie in New Hampshire. In my warm, enclosed porch, I'm sipping a cup of coffee while admiring the view of the distant snow-capped White Mountains, the thick forest bordering this rural lake, and a little knot of public safety officials. They're busily working around a hole in the ice where about a half dozen of my neighbors and four snowmobiles crashed through, into the dark and frigid water last night.

It's a pretty sight.

Very satisfying.

And my coffee is made just the way I like it, and it tastes damn good.

All in all, a nice start to the day. I'm thinking about going out for a nice long run, but I'm content to stay here and watch the goings on.

I take another sip, watch a second tow truck gingerly back its way to the open hole. A man dressed in a tan padded jumpsuit guides the way, looking for cracks and fissures. A State Police diver bobs in the center of the open water.

There are three shapes under gray wool blankets on the nearby ice. I'm sure the blankets aren't doing very much to warm them up. It's been nearly twelve hours since the snow machines and their riders went into that water. No matter what they might say to the eager news media or the grieving family, this is no longer a search and rescue.

It's just a recovery, and a damn cold one at that.

I take one more sip, raise the coffee cup in salute. "I offered you a peace treaty," I say to the silent shores. "You should have accepted."

Then there's a loud knock on the door.

Well.

Coffee cup in hand, I walk into the wide living room, still smelling of fresh paint, and I go to the merrily burning fireplace. I take a poker and stir the embers, and add a couple of chunks of dried oak, and the flames jump up, warming my face and hands.

Deep in the embers and ash are the remains of four painted signs and some orange rope. Hours earlier the signs had said DANGER! THIN ICE! But now the evidence is gone; its molecules have been transferred into smoke and ash.

I stir the fire again.

A really, really good forensics agency—perhaps the FBI or some office deep within Homeland Security—could probably come in right now and seize me and the fireplace, and through a long and intricate analysis, determine that at one point, the wood's ashes contained within belonged to painted signs.

A lot more investigation later, perhaps—and a very big perhaps— they could determine these ashes could be matched to the wood and paint of the departed signs, thereby linking me to their destruction, and the ultimate ice disaster that happened last night.

Another knock at the door.

I carefully replace the poker, reach up to the mantelpiece, take down my SIG Sauer P226 9mm pistol, and slip it into my rear waistband, under my shirt.

Perhaps this little state—my adopted home for less than a year—has access to such forensics equipment.

I start walking to my front door.

It's a doubtful prospect, but still, it's good to consider possibilities and probabilities.

I'm about twenty feet away from the front door now.

Time for possibilities, time for probabilities.

Like right now.

If there's a member of the law enforcement community on the other side of that door, I'll do my best to cooperate without being helpful.

I've grown fond of my home and have no intentions of exchanging it for a concrete and steel holding cell.

If there's a friend or neighbor of the chilly deceased at the door, well, this interesting morning is going to get a lot more interesting.

I open the door with no hesitation, and for the briefest of moments, the strong winter sun strikes my eyes, making me blink, almost making me believe in ghosts for a second. A young woman is standing on the granite steps leading into my home.

She's nearly my height, with dark black hair, almond skin, and sharp, bright brown eyes. Her hair is cut right at the shoulders, and she's wearing a black wool coat that reaches to her knees. She's also wearing black slacks, and sensible shoes for this time of year and place.

Allison.

She nods. "Owen."

"What a surprise," I say.

"A good one, I hope."

"It's . . . a surprise."

She flashes a quick smile, perfect white teeth. We go back a long way, from different hemispheres, office parks, and battlegrounds, those firing off memos or 7.62mm NATO rounds. I note her fine black wool coat has buttons down the side, but she's fastened the coat by its cloth belt, in a slipknot, easy to undo in a quick motion.

"I smell coffee," she says. "How about a cup?"

I look behind her and there's a dark-blue Chevy Marquis parked near my highway salt-stained pickup truck. She's alone.

At least I think she's alone.

There's a faint dusting of snow on the ground around the Marquis, and there's only one set of footprints: hers.

A good sign.

"Hello?" she asks. "Coffee?"

I snap back, step aside. "Come on in," I say. "I've got some fresh brewed." After the slightest of pauses, I add, "After you, Allison."

A faint smile. "Thank you, Owen. Always the gentleman."

"Most days."

She passes by and I catch a scent of lilac, and admire the sure way she walks into the room with her back toward me.

Perhaps I'm a gentleman, but I'm also a survivor.

I like Allison, I've worked with Allison, but I know if she had been ordered to, she would have followed me into my house, quickly undone her coat, drawn out a suppressor-equipped pistol and put two in the back of my head. And because I embarrassed my former employers recently, the odds aren't on my side.

# CHAPTER 2

**IN MY KITCHEN,** I silently pour her a cup of coffee, hot and black. Early on in our professional relationship, I had twice uttered the stale joke about Allison taking her coffee like she took her men. The third time I made the joke, only a quick move on my part prevented a flying ceramic mug from splitting open my forehead.

I pass her the cup and she takes it, wanders off to the porch, sipping it gently. "Nice view."

"I like it."

"Looks professional," she says. "Like someone wanted to eliminate a recurring problem or a threat without leaving a trace leading back to him." She waits. "Or her."

"Thanks for the compliment."

She says, "Maybe it was an observation, not a compliment."

"Either way, I appreciate it."

Allison turns to me. "Retirement . . . looks pretty active out there for a retirement."

"That's life in the great north woods."

"I have a job for you."

"I'm retired."

"Let me tell you about it first."

"Sure."

She takes a strong pull, holds the cup with both hands. "Do you remember a Ray Winston who worked with you in the sandbox a couple of years back?"

A smart, bulky African American from Georgia with a loud laugh, who served many years in the Army. He had a major in central Asian history and a minor in being a professional killer.

"Of course."

"He's hurt. I thought of you. He needs some help."

"What kind of help?"

"You'll see when we get there."

Ray Winston. That booming laugh. The thick, strong fingers that could easily disarm a roadside IED or make an omelet from local eggs.

"I'm retired."

"He needs your help."

"I know . . . but . . . "

I've already made up my mind, but I want to hear more from Allison. She takes another sip from her coffee, now looking at the knot of people gathered around the hole in the ice.

"Eventually they're going to come knocking on your door," she says. "Wouldn't you rather come play with me than put up with all the questions and accusations? The angry knocks on the door? The investigations? The court papers?"

"Good points," I say. "But I like this place . . . Even though I would enjoy playing with you."

"Just to be clear, I mean playing in the professional sense," Allison says, frowning. "And you never liked any place before."

"This one is different. I'm hoping it's permanent."

A tow truck starts working its winch, the strong cable emerging from the water.

"Arrangements can be made," she finally says. "Someone to stay here for a while, make sure nothing untoward happens."

A bubble of water and waves, and a red Yamaha snowmobile emerges from the water, brought up by the tow truck, swiveling slowly on the cable. A sodden shape dressed in a black snowsuit and helmet dangles from the snow machine, one foot jammed in the front.

"One more question?" I ask.

"Sure."

"Whose car are we going to take?"


I pack a small bag and join her in the kitchen, where she's washing my coffee cup and hers. She turns and wipes her hands on a towel and I say, "I'm going to need some sort of cover to bring my firearm aboard any domestic aircraft."

Allison says, "Would you like to be an air marshal?"

"I always dreamt of being a cowboy, but I guess that'll do."

She carefully folds up the towel, hangs it from the oven's long handle.

"I know what happened on your last op."

I keep quiet.

"In Serbia," she goes on.

Suddenly, it's so quiet I can hear the voices from within the frozen lake.

"Can you tell me—"

"No."

"I mean—"

"No," I say. "You know the rules."

Her coat is still fastened with the cloth belt, and I feel that she's quite close to opening the coat and removing something that will force me to talk, but that moment passes.

"Yes," she says with resignation. "I know the damn rules."

# CHAPTER 3

**OUTSIDE THE COLD** air is crisp and refreshing, and two chickadees are bouncing around a feeder I've set up near a dead birch tree. I make a mental note to make sure my future housekeeper keeps the feeders filled.

Allison heads to the Marquis, and I walk to my Ford truck. "Come on," she says. "You can ride with me."

"No, I'll follow."

"It'd be easier."

"Easier for you," I say. "But if I change my mind along the way, I want to be able to turn back and go home without jumping out."

"Your choice," she says, and opens the door to the Marquis and slides in. I admire the way her long legs straddle the edge of the car before she gets in. She catches me watching her and smiles, closing the door.

I get into my truck, give it three tries on the ignition before it starts up, and switch on the heater. Allison backs out and then I follow her up my narrow driveway, trees and brush on either side.

No offense to Allison and our lengthy relationship, but I want to minimize my risk of being in her company, in case an old enemy with a grudge tracks her down and puts an Israeli-made Spike anti-tank missile through the Marquis's hood.

From the artificial comfort of her car, she waves at me.

I wave back.

It goes along nicely until we reach the narrow state road, and a dark green New Hampshire State Police cruiser pulls across, blocking us.

I slow down and put the truck in Park. Not yet my circus, not yet my monkey. Allison waits for a moment, then opens the door and steps out.

Two bulky State Police troopers, a male and a female, emerge from the front of the cruiser and advance on Allison. In their uniforms, Sam Browne belts, holsters, weapons, and round-brimmed hats, they look like brother and sister.

A strong, no-nonsense brother and sister pair with pistols.

Allison lets them come to her, and a discussion ensues. The faces of the two troopers get redder with each passing second. One looks to the other. There's more discussion.

Allison slips a hand into her coat and I freeze—really, are you going to do something so drastic?—but no, she pulls out a cell phone. She apparently makes a phone call. Allison nods her head once, twice.

Holds the phone out.

A reluctance on the state troopers' part. Who will accept whatever message is on the other end?

The female trooper takes the lead.

She takes the phone.

Ducks her head.

Nods once, twice.

Her partner shakes his head and steps back, like he wants no part of whatever the hell is going on.

The female trooper nods once more, hands the phone over to Allison, and Allison doesn't even bother talking.

She switches the phone off and puts it back in her coat, and then turns around and walks back to the Marquis. Allison sees me and gives me a little girl wave, like some preppy young thing getting the attention of a favorite teacher.

Some pretty young thing. I wonder how many weapons she's carrying.

Allison gets back into her Marquis as the two troopers return to their cruiser, and then the cruiser backs away. The Marquis pulls out, courteously switches on its left blinker, and drives past the parked cruiser.

I follow her, and glance at the two troopers.

They are staring straight ahead, ignoring our little procession.

And I find myself smiling. It's good to be working again.

It's also good to be with Allison.

# CHAPTER 4

**IN YEARS OF** service to one's eternally grateful nation—hahaha—one thing you get used to is the dramatic pace and change of events and environments. In the morning, you could be at a sterile office in the Pentagon, and by early evening, chest-deep in some swamp in Nicaragua.

Today, for example, I roll through the day that started with snow and ice and ends with a bright winter sun in a small Georgia town called Barnes. It's about an hour west of Atlanta.

The downtown is made of white clapboard homes and three-story brick buildings, and a round grass common with the obligatory CSA veteran statue in the center. Allison drives us out to a quiet, wide road with small houses set nearby, white picket fences, and overarching trees. White and black kids bicycle up and down the smooth road, and a few play basketball at a garage with a hoop bolted to the top. Not much is going on.

Allison parks us in front of a tidy light-blue two-story home, with a front porch with a glider and two wicker chairs, and big windows. The white mailbox out front has WINSTON carefully painted on it in black letters.

From the porch, an American flag hangs limply from a small pole jutting from one of the pillars.

Allison switches off the car. Our drive from the Atlanta-Hartsfield Airport had been a quiet one, and I knew from experience that it was best not to press Allison about what was going on or what she had planned. I kept my mouth shut and she had returned the favor.

"Here we are," she says.

"Nice."

We get out and I breathe in the Georgia air and look up at the dark-blue sky, not a cloud blocking anything. Allison comes around the car. She's dumped her heavy winter coat for a light-blue blazer that fits her well and does a good job of concealing her weaponry.

"What are you looking at?" she asks.

"The sky."

"What's up there?"

"The little specks of airliners full of men and women in first class, sipping on their drinks, working on their papers or laptops, ignoring what they call 'flyover country.' They never quite care or understand that flyover country produces most of the fighting men and women who go out and bleed on their behalf."

"You get all that from looking at the sky?"

I smile at her. "I've had practice."

She goes to the picket fence, opens the gate, and lets me through. I sense we're being watched from inside. "What can you tell me about Ray Winston?" she asks.

"Ray? Big as an East German car, tough, moves quickly and quietly.

He can snap a sentry's neck or break through a front door and terrorize a Taliban squad with just his voice."

I pause, memories getting unpacked from little boxes in the back of my mind. They're demanding attention. I try not to give it to them.

"Go on," she says.

"He's smart, too," I say. "When we were in Iraq, he could talk about Babylon and Ur and make it interesting. The same in Afghanistan. He loved talking about Alexander the Great. He'd say, 'Imagine that cat Alexander, marching all the way to this cold and dry place, and for what?'"

"Sounds like a one of a kind."

"One of the strongest, bravest, and smartest guys I ever served with."

Allison walks ahead of me and I join her on the porch. Before she opens the door, she says to me in a voice that's slightly bleak, "Hold that thought, will you?"

I do, because I don't know what to say.

Allison opens the door and we walk in, and I catch the pungent odor right away.

The smell of someone dying.

# CHAPTER 5

**THERE'S A SMALL** entryway to the front and what seems to be a formal dining room to the right, but Allison expertly steers us to the left. In a few seconds, I take it all in. The room had once been a living room or a parlor or whatever the hell you want to call it, but the two couches and three chairs have been pushed aside to make room for the large hospital bed in the center.

There's a *whir-click* of a ventilator and I slowly walk forward. There's a crumpled shape underneath the covers. I force myself to move on. I'm no stranger to the battlefield or medic tents or evac helicopters, but there's still something bone-jarring about seeing what's left after the fighting is over. It can make you ill, right down to the marrow.

An African American man is asleep on the bed, his face swollen and sallow. A ventilator tube comes out from his throat and down to a machine. An oxygen tube with twin openings is around his nostrils. His left eye socket is empty and gaping. His right arm is on top of the light-blue cotton blanket, monitor devices clipped to the end of the fingers.

There's no left arm.

Based on the shape under the blanket, there are no legs, either.

A plastic bag dangling underneath the bed is half full of urine.

On the walls are framed photographs of this man as a baby, child, and adolescent. Two of him in a football uniform, one high school, the other college.

There's another framed photograph of him in a uniform, Army this time, and a pretty African American woman is pinning a Ranger tab to his upper arm. Both are smiling, and he looks confident enough to take on the world at breakfast and relax in the afternoon with a good cigar and a snifter of Rémy Martin.

I'm at his side. Allison is quiet in the corner.

I'm thinking a lot, but there's also fury building up inside of me, wanting to make Allison take me back to the airport, so I could be on the ground a day later, back in the 'Stan, looking to kill everyone and anyone who did this to him. Then I'd kill their flocks and flatten their homes.

Just like Alexander the Great.

The sole eyelid flickers open, and the eye moves around, focuses, and snaps onto me.

The man smiles.

"Hey, Top, good to see you," he says in a voice so soft it's hard to hear.

I touch his forehead, blink my eyes. "Good to see you, too, Ray."

"Liar," he whispers.

"If so, you taught me," I say. "You were always the best at flinging tales around. You still think Alexander invaded Afghanistan just because he was horny and wanted to spread his seed?"

The smile widens and for that sight alone, I would gratefully sign over my entire checking account to whoever wanted it.

"You think he marched all the way from warm Greece with all those fine chicks and wine to go to the 'Stan only for gold and glory? Don't make sense, man . . ."

His eyelid flutters and closes again. His voice is lower. "Don't make sense, man . . ."

My fists are clenched very tight. He falls back asleep.

The woman from the photograph walks into the room. Marilyn, I recall. Marilyn. She has on black open-toed high-heeled shoes, tight jeans, and a white pullover top with the sleeves rolled up on her arms, the front showing a hint of cleavage. Her toenails and fingernails both have bright red nail polish on them, and there's gold jewelry on her fingers and wrists.

Her skin is mahogany and flawless, and her ink-colored hair is pulled back in a simple ponytail. With her looks and style, she could easily be a runway model, save for two things: she's just a tad too short and her brown eyes are staring at me with a mix of fury and disdain.

Marilyn says to Allison, "This him?"

"It's him."

"Doesn't look like much."

Marilyn goes to her husband and touches his forehead, checking the readouts on the ventilator and looking over the medical supplies on the nightstand.

I gently clear my throat. "Ma'am, however I look, I can do whatever needs to get done."

She nearly spits the words out.

"We'll see about that."

Allison is near me, like she's ready to take some of the brunt from the angry Marilyn. "How's he doing today?"

"Not much change," she says, bustling around the nightstand. "He drifts off too much . . . sleeps too much . . . and those damn dreams."

I say, "Shouldn't he be in a VA hospital, or some intensive care unit?"

Marilyn drops a tube of ointment and says sharply, "You trying to tell me how to take care of my man?"

"No, it's just that I know it can be overwhelming and—"

She looks me up and down, and for a few ugly seconds I feel like I'm back at basic, facing my first drill sergeant. "You've been here exactly ninety seconds and you know shit, that's what you know."

I nod. "You're absolutely right. My apologies. No disrespect, ma'am."

She stares and stares, and then picks up the tube she dropped. "Stop calling me ma'am, all right? Sounds like we're at a church meeting or something."

Marilyn puts some ointment on two fingers and gently applies it to Ray's lips. "Thing is, the hospital, they do their best, but I'm not interested in them doing their best. I want things to be above and beyond. So I took Ray out of there and brought him here, thinking being home would help him bounce back faster, with me and the home health aides. Hasn't happened yet, but it will. I know it will."

I say, "Ma'am . . ." and then correct myself, and say, "Marilyn, I served two tours with Ray. I'm here to help in any way I can. What do you want?"

She says, "Allison, you didn't tell him?"

"No," she says. "I thought it would be better coming from you."

"Fair enough," Marilyn says. Those hard brown eyes are now boring right into me. "I want you to find the person responsible for doing this to my Raynie. The one who hurt him so bad. And I want payback."

I look at the sleeping man, hard to contrast *this* Ray with the Ray I knew back then, who was among the best in my unit. "Allison is probably your best bet there," I say. "I can talk to Ray, and if Allison and I can get good intel on when and exactly where this happened in Afghanistan, that'd be a start. Allison could locate the exact group who did this, put in a word, run it through the chain of command and the targeting officers—"

Marilyn laughs, interrupts me. "Damn, girl, I guess you didn't tell him anything, did you?"

Allison seems suddenly interested in the view outside.

Ray's wife says, "It wasn't the Taliban who did this. Or al-Qaeda. Or ISIS." When I look puzzled, Marilyn gestures to the other room. "If you want to find out more, come with me. Both of you."

She leaves and I don't hesitate.

I walk right behind her.

# CHAPTER 6

**THE OTHER ROOM** is the exact size of the one where Ray lies, but is much more cluttered. The walls are colored light-blue and pink, and there's a baby crib and bassinet in one corner, and two mobiles on the ceiling of little plastic birds and pigs circling in the strong Georgia sun.

Marilyn sees the look on my face and says, "Ray was promised a training command here in Georgia, after his last tour. Then we were going to . . . well, we waited too long."

There's a couch with a pillow and some blankets piled up, and I can see this hard and beautiful wife, dozing here when she can, waking up instantly at the slightest sound and murmur from the next room. There's a crowded bookshelf against the wall, piles of magazines on the floor, a light-brown mini-fridge, and a wide-screen television. Marilyn pushes aside some of the blankets and sits down on the couch. Allison joins her.

There's no other seating in the room.

I keep on standing.

Marilyn picks up the remote, and pressing a button, says, "Just watch."

The television flickers to life and a shaky recording fills the screen, featuring a very familiar-looking television correspondent named Jack Zach. He's about twenty years older than me and a bit less defined, with a thick white beard that under the right light and angle makes him look like Ernest Hemingway to Jack's more breathless and dumber contemporaries.

Something I know Jack Zach has never discouraged.

He whispers, "I'm special field correspondent Jack Zach, filing this report under very dangerous circumstances." Then he continues speaking about this dangerous outpost of America's will . . . the daily mortar attacks . . . vicious attempts . . . deadly area . . . hotbed of terrorism . . . incubator of hatred against the West . . . and I tune out everything he's saying and just look.

He's dressed in a blue helmet, dark-blue Kevlar vest with PRESS imprinted on it in white letters—as if any of these local Pashtun tribesmen would even know or care what the word meant—and a camouflage jacket that's not Army issue. As he talks, the camera shows footage of the FOB—forward operating base—where he and his meager crew are located.

I start remembering the highlights (and mostly lowlights) of his career. Starting off as a local New York TV correspondent, he did some groundbreaking stories about police and gangs, then did a stretch for one of the three big networks, and then started bouncing around after that.

There was the radio talk show, the television talk show, a couple of reality-television programs, lots of gossip tales about his fights and marriages, and articles on *Page Six* and in *People*. Now he's a roaming correspondent for the latest scrappy cable news network. From the looks of it, he creates his own videos and then decides whether to submit them. I have an itching feeling that this one never made it to press.

The footage continues with Jack interviewing the FOB commander and some of the guys in the field. There's lots of joshing and back-slapping, and finally, in a five-second shot, I see Ray Winston, all decked out in full battle rattle, watching the circus going on.

"There's my Raynie," Marilyn whispers. "Don't my boy look good?"

Then there's a few seconds of jerky camera work as two mortar rounds explode outside of the FOB perimeter. Some shots of bombs being dropped from an American B-52 quickly follow and there's one last glamour shot in front of a sandbag-covered building with an American flag draped near the doorway where Jack looks into the camera and says nothing of substance.

Marilyn pauses the action on the screen, and now it comes to me.

"Jack Zach," I say. "He said something or reported something he shouldn't have. Classified or operational plans. Information that allowed the Taliban to attack and hurt Ray and the others. Am I right?"

Allison looks uncomfortable and if anything, the anger and fury in Marilyn's eyes increase.

"No, Owen," she says. "You're wrong."

"Then why are you showing me this?"

Her hand goes back to the remote. "You're about to find out. It's worse than anything you can imagine. Much, much worse."

# CHAPTER 7

**THE IMAGE ON** the big-screen television comes back to life, and Marilyn works the buttons and *zip-zip-zip* we fast-forward through some similar shots.

Something starts tickling along the back of my arms and my neck.

Jack Zach is back on the screen, and there's more mindless talking, but it's a shushed type of talking, because Jack isn't embedded with the Army, my buds, and Ray Winston anymore.

He's embedded with a group of Taliban fighters, moving with them among the rocks and hills and gullies, and he and his cameraman film a three-man crew operating a Russian-made 82mm Podnoss mortar. They drop in three projectiles and Jack whispers as his cameraman follows the trajectory . . .

. . . right to the FOB where Jack had previously been.

I whisper, "I'll be damned."

The FOB suffers two direct hits on the compound, and then the mortar crew, the other Taliban, and Jack Zach scurry away, and—

It's nighttime. The scenes are being filmed in ghostly green night vision.

They're by a road.

More whispered reporting from Jack Zach. Three Taliban members are carrying what looks to be an artillery shell and they start burying it at the side of the road.

Good God.

When the three are done, they move back and Jack goes with them. They're in a gully now, peering over, looking at the road.

Lights in the distance.

A small convoy is approaching.

Ray's wife then whispers, "They weren't supposed to be there. But they were ordered to do it . . . ordered to get ambushed."

I feel like I might just get sick to my stomach.

Jack's whispers get more urgent as the vehicles approach. There are up-armored Humvees and two trucks, and Jesus God, can't somebody warn them, can't they see the IED buried before them, won't Jack do something and—

A loud explosion, ball of light overwhelms the night vision gear. The camera shakes and there are the exulted shouts of the Taliban crew. As gunfire erupts, there's a quick shot of burning overturned vehicles.

Then Allison speaks up. "I think we've seen enough."

Marilyn says, "No, you haven't." So the three of us sit there and watch the fighting. We watch the wounded and dying go on, and see the American soldiers fall, while an American correspondent watches.

# CHAPTER 8

**WHEN THE TELEVISION** is switched off, I say, "When did this happen?"

"Six months ago," Allison says. "Didn't you hear about it?"

A half year ago, I was just getting settled into the lakeside home I'd dreamed about forever, so I say, "No. Back then I wasn't watching the news, or reading any newspapers."

Marilyn carefully puts the remote down on a coffee table. "Jack Zach did nothing," she says. "He's an American and was embedded with Ray's unit. He did a couple of stories with them, pretended to be their friend . . . and then went to the Taliban a week later to watch his own get killed and wounded."

I say, "I'm sure this caused one hell of a firestorm when it broke."

Marilyn crosses her arms. "Sure. Except no one knew that Jack Zach had been there, what he had known. No one knew that he could've stopped them . . . All the while my Raynie is barely alive, crapping in a bedpan, peeing into a tube, screaming every night from the memories. Two of his friends were killed. Three others were wounded. He and the others in that unit were forgotten."

It's now clear.

"What can I do?" I ask.

Marilyn's voice is crisp and clear. "You find this Jack Zach, and for what he did to my man . . . and the others . . . I want you to hurt him. I want him destroyed. I want him . . . gone."

Not much to say after that. There's a moan from the next room, and Marilyn disappears.

Allison says, "Well."

"I . . . What the hell is this?"

She waits.

I say, "You bring me all the way here to Georgia to see my old bud, and for what?"

Allison says, "I've known you . . . for when it counts. I've read your after-action reports. I've gotten verbal debriefings—with no official records—of other activities you've done. That's why you're here."

"Really? You think you know me that well, that I'd put my butt on the line, do something so wildly illegal? I'd like to remind you, I'm retired."

"I know that, but—"

"And I'd also like to remind you that back home in New Hampshire, I'm now on law enforcement's radar for a little lake accident that happened last night. Do you think me stepping out on a revenge mission is the right thing to do?"

Marilyn comes back in, wiping her hands on two pieces of tissue. "Ray always spoke highly of you, Owen. Always. And now . . . you see what they did to him. And not a thing has happened to this Jack Zach. Hell, I wouldn't have even known about all this if someone hadn't anonymously dropped off that DVD in my mailbox. Are you just going to let this go?"

I make sure she and Allison are looking me square in the eyes. "That was then, this is now. You both think I'm going to ride out on this personal mission of vengeance . . . this revenge? Is that what you think? Is that who you think I am?"

Another moan from the other room, but Marilyn and Allison don't move, don't respond.

I give them both a reassuring smile.

"You're right," I say. "That's exactly what I'm going to do."

# CHAPTER 9

**ANOTHER DAY, ANOTHER** transition.

Instead of the frozen Lake Marie in New Hampshire or the pleasant warmth of Barnes, Georgia, I'm in the urban wilderness of Manhattan.

But at least I'm not alone.

I'm sitting in a bland dark-blue GMC Yukon, with Allison sitting in the driver's seat. Earlier, I had made a motion to drive, but she'd given me a "Nice try, bud" look and slid right in. We had spent the previous night at a faceless airport hotel outside of the Atlanta-Hartsfield Airport, and when we had landed at JFK, Allison led me through a series of walkways and blank corridors, until we came upon a fenced-in parking area where a quick flash of a slim leather wallet to the lot's attendant gave us access to a Yukon.

"Quite the big vehicle for such a slim lady," I pointed out.

She said, "Had to make sure we had enough room for your ass and ego. Get the hell in."

Now we're illegally parked along Fifth Avenue, a block north of St. Patrick's Cathedral, near Rockefeller Plaza, and waiting. A light mist is falling and a low cloud cover obscures the upper floors of the surrounding buildings. I check the dashboard clock. Not quite time.

I'm wearing a suit that sixty-three minutes earlier had been hanging off a rack. My SIG Sauer pistol is in its holster, underneath the front seat. I'm hoping I'm not going to need it in the next hour or so.

Allison looks reasonably calm, letting the lines of honking traffic and fast-moving pedestrians flow around us, but I'm jittery. Too many cars, too many people, too much movement.

I find my eyes go from the windshield to the side windows to the side-view mirror and back again. For the third time this morning, an NYPD police cruiser pulls up behind us, lights flashing.

And for the third time, Allison ignores it.

She says, "You sure you want to do it this way?"

I'm still looking at the police car. The cop on the passenger's side is speaking into a radio microphone, no doubt running our license plate. "Sometimes the direct approach works best. Surprises people, knocks them off balance."

"Sometimes the direct approach is suicidal," she says. "Back in the day, tribal warriors would directly charge the British in South Africa. Very direct, very brave, except when they ran up against the Brits' Maxim machine guns. Not a happy outcome for the warriors."

"If I see any Redcoats, I'll come right back."

"I'm sure you will."

"And then you can comfort me about how close I came to my demise."

"Don't hold your breath."

The NYPD cruiser switches off its lights, backs up, and slips into traffic. I check the clock one more time. Six more minutes.

We sit in silence.

I say, "Lousy day."

Allison leans, peers out the side window. "I love this kind of weather."

"Why?"

She sits back. "Cloud cover like this means airliners can't run into skyscrapers." She taps her fingers and then says, "Okay. Time."

I reach for the door and then stop. Allison's hand is on my wrist.

This is the first time she's ever touched me in a way that doesn't involve threatening me or tossing me on my ass during a training exercise.

"Owen."

"Still here."

"Please . . . about your last op, with Emily and the others. Can you tell me—"

I reach over and gently—oh so gently—remove her hand from my wrist. "You know I can't say a word."

Allison says, "So it's just the official story, then?"

I give her hand a gentle squeeze, place it down on her lap. "Always the official story, you know that."

# CHAPTER 10

**IT'S JUST PAST** noon, which means it's lunchtime, and the building's lobby is busy, with people coming out and in. I stride through the masses confidently, as if I belong, as if I know exactly where I'm going.

There are waist-high security kiosks where employees or vendors flash their ID cards at the automatic reader, and, moving briskly, I "tailgate" a fast-moving guy carrying a cardboard coffee caddy with four containers.

There's a momentary beep, but within seconds, I'm in an elevator car, heading up.

I'm in the elevator for just over a minute, and it's comforting to be in this crowded car, with men and women who are white, Asian, Hispanic, African American, and who knows what else, all riding together in peace.

It's a nice microcosm of what isn't working in the world anymore.

The elevator stops at the twenty-ninth floor, the door slides open, and out I go.

The carpeted lobby area is wide and luxurious, with bright shining letters on the far wall over the receptionist area that read:

INTERNATIONAL NEWS NETWORK. Three large televisions hang from the ceiling, all showing the current news footage from INN, and there are seven poster-sized photos of INN correspondents along the curved walls, three showing Jack Zach out in the field, with his thick white beard and seemingly merry blue eyes.

I'm thinking those eyes would look mighty fine swollen and blackened.

The desk is curved, and an attractive blond woman is sitting behind it, wearing a headset. I walk up and she smiles up at me with cool efficiency and says, "May I help you?"

I smile right back. She's just a foot soldier, a grunt, a flak catcher, and I'm going to do my best not to harm her in any way. She has on a bright-red dress and has a little yellow sunflower tattooed on the back of her right wrist.

"Yes," I say.

I don't go on, and she looks just slightly puzzled. "And . . . how can I help you, sir?"

"I'm here to see Jack Zach."

"Oh." Her fingers tap on a computer keyboard and she says, "Do you have an appointment?"

"No."

"I . . . well . . ."

I step closer, still smiling. "You see, I met Jack overseas. When I was serving. In some pretty nasty situations."

"Oh."

I nod. "And things were getting pretty hairy, and when it was done, Jack said, 'Bud, anytime you get to the city, look me up.'"

I make a point of surveying the lobby area. "What a place. Hell of a lot better than desert and mountains. So can I see him, please?"

"Can I have your name?"

"Thanks," I say without answering her, and I walk away and take a seat on a comfortable couch. The young receptionist turns and I see her lips moving as she talks to someone. There are two heavy glass doors on either side of her desk, and INN employees coming in use a keycard to get access to the floor.

I don't have a keycard.

No worries.

I pick up a copy of today's *New York Times* and pretend to read.

A few minutes pass and the young woman says, "Sir?"

"That's me."

"I'm afraid Jack Zach's not here."

"Oh. Can you tell me where he is?"

"I'm afraid not," she says, giving me a sympathetic look, though I can also tell that she hopes I'll get up and leave.

*Sorry,* I think.

"Gee, that's all right," I say, returning to the *Times*. "I'll wait until he comes back."

"I don't know if he's going to be here today."

"That's okay. I'll wait."

"But . . . you'll have to leave, then."

"Thanks for your concern," I say. "But I like it here. You know why?"

She shakes her head.

"No goddamn sand fleas." I pause. "Ma'am."

Time slides by and as people come in and out, I say to every one of them, "Excuse me, will you tell Jack I'm here? Will you tell him I'm waiting? Please?"

Some of the INN workers ignore me, others just give a nod or a smile, and several others raise an eyebrow to the receptionist. Finally, it happens.

The door to the left opens with a heavy buzz and two large men come out, dressed in black shoes, dark-blue slacks, white shirts with black ties, and dark-blue blazers. Both of them have an earpiece and both are just a year or two younger than me.

No red coats, which I guess is a good thing.

I gently fold the newspaper and replace it on the coffee table.

I stand up.

"Gosh, neither one of you looks like Jack Zach," I say.

"Yeah, we get that often," the one on the left says. "You going to make this easy?"

"Define easy."

"You turn around and walk out."

I smile at the receptionist, and she gives me a weak smile in response.

"Never liked it easy," I say. "So why start now?"

# CHAPTER 11

**BUT THEN I** decide to make it simple for the fellows, since there are eye-witnesses around. I step away from the couch, so each can flank me and seize an arm.

They fold my arms behind me and start walking. I go right along with them, even though, if I was in the mood, I could have thrown both of them on the floor and given them three broken bones apiece.

Lucky for them I wasn't in the mood.

The receptionist buzzes the left door open for the two guys, and I'm pushed through. We go down a carpeted hallway, and make a sharp left through an unmarked metal door. The hallway is no longer carpeted, but bare concrete.

We move right along, past supply rooms, a break area, and a small kitchen, and end up in front of what looks to be a service elevator. Their hands are still firmly on my wrists, and with a push of a button, the door grumbles open. I'm pushed inside.

Dumb.

With only a few seconds' work, both of these men could have been bundled in the elevator ahead of me with bleeding noses.

But I was being Mister Cooperative in front of INN employees, so I go in the elevator and the door slides closed.

"You know where Jack Zach is?"

They both keep quiet.

There are no buttons in the elevator. It's probably a straight shot right to the ground floor.

"You sure?"

One of the guys says, "Why do you want to see Jack Zach?"

I say, "He owes me five bucks."

I can see them in the mirrored inside of the elevator. One of them smirks and the other one—with a very finely trimmed mustache and tiny closed-in ears—pulls my right arm up with a sharp tug and says, "This is a professional operation, okay? You get out of here, and you don't come back. Just go the hell away."

"But Jack invited me to come visit."

He twists my arm again and I think he's disappointed that I don't cry out. He says, "You don't have fine legs, long hair, or nice boobs, so forget it."

"Maybe you'll change your mind if you get to know me."

The elevator shudders to a stop, the door opens, and we emerge out onto a loading dock with bare concrete and overhead fluorescent light. We go through an open bay with a rolling, metal garage door and into a narrow alleyway with trash bins. Then I'm shoved and I make a big scene of falling down.

The guy on my left says, "Seth, you didn't have to do that."

Seth says, "He was pissing me off. I wanted to show him I meant business."

I get up, brush off my hands, and smile. "Hey, I understand. You guys have an important job to do, you're on the front line of protecting Jack Zach and other employees."

"You got that right," the second guard says.

I smile widely, walk over to him, and extend a hand. The light mist is still falling and I can make out the sounds of Midtown traffic roaring by. "No hard feelings, okay?"

He smiles back at me and thinking he's won, and being gracious, I suppose, he accepts my handshake.

At least his third mistake of the day.

I grab his hand, twist it, pull him forward and off balance, and with my free hand, slam it hard against his nose. He cries out and I whip him around, and then slam him into the concrete side of the building, kick out his legs from underneath him, and push him to the ground, tugging his suit coat down so he can't move his arms.

His partner's eyes are wide and he's scrambling to get something from under his coat, and I spin out and kick his legs out from under him, and he falls on his back. I stand over him and gently put my foot on his throat. His eyes are bulging.

"I like you, so I'll make it quick," I say, pressing down some with each word. "Do you know where Jack Zach is?"

He closes his eyes, like he doesn't want to remember seeing me. I can't say I blame him. "Please, bud, how the hell should I know? I just work security."

I press down harder. "But there are rumors. Words get passed around. Am I right?"

His face reddens. "Man . . . do you think a shithead like him talks to guys like me? Please . . ."

I'm about to assert more force on his throat when there's a shout of "Freeze!" behind me, and I turn.

It's Allison, holding a Beretta 9mm in her hands, pointing right at me, and for the briefest of moments, I think, *yep, this has been one long ruse to get me here and eliminate a problem* . . .

She lowers the pistol. I take a good breath. I should know better. Allison . . . she's done a lot of things, she'll do a lot of things, but she'd never bring Ray and Marilyn Winston into her dealings.

She pulls out a pair of handcuffs and secures my hands behind my back.

"Move," she says to me. To the guards on the ground she says, "Sorry, guys. We'll be around later to get your statements."

We slip out of the alleyway.

Back in the Yukon, after she's uncuffed my arms, she starts driving. "How did you know they'd dump you out there?"

"Corporations want to keep things quiet," I say, rubbing my wrists. "So no front lobby exit for troublemakers." We come to a stop at an intersection, and a bicycle courier zips through without stopping. "So why the pistol and handcuffs?"

The light changes to green and Allison surges ahead, passing white delivery trucks and yellow taxis. "I wanted the guards to see someone take you in. They'll think the cops are taking care of things."

I say, "Gee, aren't we working well together?"

"Don't push it," she says. "Why did you want to make a scene back there?"

She's driving so fast now that my right hand is clutching the overhead bar. "I want Jack Zach to know we're coming after him. If he thinks it's funny, he'll underestimate us. If he's concerned, he might move, and if he moves, we've got him."

A flick of her wrist and we pass down a middle lane, barely scraping by two cabs. Horns blare. "And when we get him?"

"One thing at a time, one thing at a time," I say. "Right now, think of Ernest Hemingway."

"Why? Being with you right now is fulfilling my macho man quotient."

"Gosh, that's sweet," I say. "And don't tease me when it comes to the great Papa. Even he had a support staff, someone fetching him whiskey and typewriter ribbons. Let's find Jack's."

# CHAPTER 12

**AFTER FORTY-NINE MINUTES,** which Allison has spent on the phone, talking and researching, we're in New Rochelle, New York. It's home to Walt Cooper, a nine-year veteran cameraman for Jack Zach. He lives in a wide two-story house made of brick and white clapboard, and as we exit the Yukon, Allison says, "I'll take the lead."

"Why?"

"Because on our ride out here, I found the info. Finders, interrogators."

"All right," I say. "But if things get too tense, feel free to hold my hand."

"Only if I feel like snapping a finger or two."

The yard is well kept, and there are two pink children's bicycles tangled up near the hedges.

Allison rings the front doorbell, and a woman in her early thirties answers. This is Walt's wife, Rachel. She's what people call pleasingly plump and has ginger hair and a friendly look. She's wearing a checked flannel shirt and jeans. Allison says that we once worked with Walt, and with a smile that no one can turn down, asks to be invited in.

We sit in a cozy living room with framed photos of twin girls—the latest shows them at about ten years of age—and of cameraman Walt

Cooper out in the field, a few with the famed Jack Zach. After we sit down, Rachel politely interrupts Allison.

"You think that in one of his overseas assignments, Walt may have filmed a terrorist leader? By accident?"

Allison says, "That's correct. I always thought that Walt was one of the good guys. Since Jack Zach's been exposed in a negative light lately, some of his cameramen are sharing evidence to support those assumptions."

"And you think Walt has this evidence . . . from where?"

"In Beirut, late last year. After a car bomb went off, Walt filmed the aftermath. Most of what he taped didn't make it on air. That's the footage we're interested in examining, recordings of the crowds gathered around the crater and debris. If you can tell us where he is now, we'll talk to him directly."

"But why not go after Jack Zach himself?" she asks.

Allison says, "Jack Zach is . . . Jack Zach. He's not exactly going to turn himself in. We think we'd have a more successful outcome by talking to your husband directly."

"I see," she says, one hand removing a bit of invisible lint from her left leg. "I also see what you're up to. It's pretty clear. I don't know why you're trying to get information from me about Walt and Jack, but I won't do it. And I won't put you in contact with my husband, either."

"Ma'am," I say.

"Let me finish."

"Of course."

Rachel holds her hands together. "I don't know who you are and how you work, but my husband and Jack and his producers . . . they're a very loyal, tight-knit team, always looking out for one another. Jack is a jerk, a blowhard, a prima donna, and frankly, a pain in the ass to be around. But he treats Walt right. And the rest of his team."

She stands up. "Please leave. And don't bother me again. I wish you people knew the kind of loyalty I'm talking about."

Allison wants to talk but I interrupt her and say, "We completely understand, ma'am. Our apologies for disturbing you."

I really want to say something else but I keep my counsel. I'm in this nice living room, but for some reason, I'm hearing the *whir-click* of the respirator from Georgia. We walk out the front door and I poke around in my new suit, pull out a slip of paper describing the kind of cloth that went into making it, and I write a phone number on the back.

"Here," I say. "My cell. If you change your mind . . . or anything comes up, please call me."

"Don't worry," she says, "I won't."

But she doesn't toss the paper away in front of me, which I hope is a good sign.

Allison and I treat ourselves to dinner that evening. For dessert, we split a rich, decadent chocolate mousse, and after three bites she says, "You were pushy back there, getting us out of the Coopers' house."

"I didn't want her to get mad at us," I say, "and I didn't want to get mad at her."

"Mad at us, I can understand. It's always a good idea to leave room for cooperation down the road. But mad at her? For what?"

"Because of what she said, about loyalty. I . . . I was afraid I was going to say something inappropriate, something that might have gotten back to Jack Zach."

"Like what?"

"Like tell her that loyalty is what *we're* doing for Ray and his wife Marilyn. The two of them suffering back there in Georgia. That's loyalty . . . I wanted to tell her that we absolutely knew what that means."

I examine our bill and slide out cash to pay for it. Cash doesn't leave easily accessible or traceable records.

It's late so we take the hotel's glass elevator up to the thirty-fifth floor. I notice the presence of my SIG Sauer under my new suit. I go with Allison as she unlocks her door and she turns and says, "I'm all right."

"I know you are, but I still want to make sure."

So I pass by her and go into her room—modeled exactly like mine with a king-size bed and a cherrywood desk in the corner—and when I've checked the corners and turn toward my room, I see Allison sitting on the edge of her bed.

Her blazer is off and there are no weapons visible but I'm sure they're around.

Her blouse fits her snugly and I can't help but admire her body. It's toned and lethal, from hours of training.

Her hair looks loose and more relaxed than earlier. I don't know what she did to it during my quick survey of her room, but I know that I like what I see.

She looks up at me, gently crosses her legs at the ankles, drawing my attention to her high heels, which are still on her feet. Then she leans back on the bed, resting on her hands.

She says, "Everything okay?"

I'm standing in front of her, and I surprise myself when my hand traces her smooth cheek.

"Everything's fine," I say.

She closes her eyes. "Not that I need your protection, you understand."

My hand is still on that smooth skin. I wonder how it tastes.

"I understand completely," I say. "Until then . . ."

She presses her cheek against my fingertips.

"Until then," she says, opening her eyes.

Then I leave and close the door behind me.

# CHAPTER 13

**AFTER SHOWERING, SHAVING,** and getting dressed the next morning, I hear a knock at the door. SIG Sauer pistol in hand, I approach the door and say, "Yes?"

"It's Allison."

"Hold on."

There's a peephole in the door but I know from experience and training that I shouldn't use it. All it would take is someone with an ice pick to ruin your day. You might also open the door just enough to keep the security chain fastened, but a shotgun barrel could still fit through the gap, with a blast that could cut you in half.

Earlier, I had maneuvered a bathroom mirror to see out in the hallway when the door is open, and when I look, Allison is standing by herself, two dark-brown paper coffee cups in her hands.

I undo the chain, put the SIG Sauer in my rear waistband, and let her in. She's wearing what looks to be the same outfit as yesterday but is managing to do so without a single wrinkle or errant fold. As she comes in, I watch her long legs move nicely under the snug skirt, her calf muscles flexing as she walks.

She passes a cup to me and I close the door behind her. Allison raises her cup in salute and says, "I know where Walt Cooper is, and therefore, Jack Zach."

"Where?"

"The refugee camp in Karkamis, on the Turkey–Syria border. Jack's there, filming a story, with his trusty cameraman Walt Cooper along."

"Good job," I say, taking a satisfying sip and appreciating that Allison has ordered it the way I like it. "Where did you get that from?"

She moves through my room to my cherrywood desk and matching chair. She sits down and says, "A nice, lengthy phone call between hubby and wife."

I go and sit on my bed, which I made out of military habit, and notice that the little spark I felt last night isn't gone.

It's definitely not forgotten.

And from the way she's averting her gaze here and there, it's not forgotten by Allison, either.

I say, "I thought you folks weren't supposed to spy on Americans."

She smiles, takes a sweet swallow from her coffee. "We don't."

"Really?"

"Uh-huh. We might read their emails, listen to their phone calls, intercept their overseas mail, but we never, ever spy on them. It's against the law, you know."

"Yes, and in all our time together, I've always known how much you respect the law."

"Disrespect doesn't mean I get to go AWOL," she says.

"Point taken."

I say, "So how long are Jack and Walt going to be at the refugee camp?"

"Not sure," she says. "There's a big city nearby called Gaziantep. You'll fly into the airport there, get transportation to the refugee camp, which is about seventy-four klicks away."

"Can you arrange the travel?"

"Airlines, sure. On the ground . . . I'd prefer you to be on your own. If things go south . . ."

"Yeah, no connection to you or Uncle Sam."

"But I can get you traveling with a disposable cover. That agreeable?"

Traveling with no cover means you go as yourself and on your own, nothing there to back you up in a crisis. Going with a cover means that you've got papers and a passport saying you're, let's say, a wheat expert from the US Department of Agriculture, and the government will stick by you even if it makes them blue in the face.

A disposable cover is similar, except under intense scrutiny from the bad guys (or good guys that are pissed at you), it can collapse. Your papers and passport will be held against you as the work of dark money and black chicanery, and not the product of any official government system.

Still, it's better than nothing.

"I'll take it," I say.

"Good, because that's all I got," she says. "Except there's one more thing. You got a pen on you?"

"Aw, you giving me your personal number?"

From her sidebag—never call it a purse—she tosses me a silver pen. Allison doesn't take the bait. She says, "Use it when you have to."

I slip it into a pants pocket. "Yes ma'am."

I go to the end of bed, pick up my bag, and start to pack.

"And if you run into Jack Zach over there, what's your plan?" she asks.

"To show him the error of his ways," I say, zipping open side pockets.

"Besides that," she says.

"Why don't you come along and find out?"

She shakes her head. "Can't go."

"Good decision," I say. "The border between Turkey and Syria can be a tricky and hairy place. Makes sense for you to stay behind."

Her eyes narrow so fast she almost looks feline . . . and one angry feline at that. "I'll have you know that at four p.m. today, I'm taking part in an intelligence briefing at the White House. If it wasn't for that, I'd be right next to you."

And like an angry cat, she spits out one last word: "Owen."

# CHAPTER 14

**IT TOOK NEARLY** a full day of travel and eventually, I'm on a bus from Gaziantep to the refugee camp. It's mostly a four-lane road with signs in Arabic and English. We pass through a landscape of barren hills, low brush, and trees.

It's been a long day, which I've spent planning, because through Allison's work, I found out that I had a contact waiting for me at the Karkamis refugee camp. It's someone I'd known in my previous life.

When we're about thirty minutes out from Karkamis, I see the Turkish military keeping a wary eye on their neighbors just to the south, because usually, they like to tear each other into bloody pieces. There are small contingents of troops near the highway's exits and a number of Turkish-made AVC-15 armored combat vehicles.

Aboard the bus are a very few tourists, camera crews from Japan and Australia, some UN relief officials, and two guys with ill-fitting civilian clothes and close-cropped blond hair speaking Russian. They took note of me when I got on the bus. I did the same of them, and we acknowledged each other's background with the briefest of nods. We silently said, "You stay out of my way, I'll stay out of yours," which was agreeable.

As we get closer to Karkamis, the traffic slows. There are white tents all around us as far as you can see, stretching out to the horizons. Our bus wheezes to a halt at a temporary shelter made of concrete blocks and metal roofs. We step into the mild December temperatures, surrounded by the sound of engines and horns, and people talking and shouting. Over everything, the smell of diesel, cigarette smoke, and despair exudes from tens of thousands of people living on the edge.

Following the directions supplied by Allison, I walk past another collection of white tents with the blue UN seal and the letters UNHCR stenciled on each. I continue along full clotheslines, outdoor cooking fires tended by exhausted-looking women, kids playing soccer, men in chairs playing dominoes, drinking coffee, and smoking. It's the most chaotic thing I've ever seen.

I'm carrying an overnight bag and my SIG Sauer is in a waist holster, and my identification says I'm a member of the US State Department's Bureau of Security. If things go badly, my fake ID will be my first line of defense and my SIG Sauer will be my second and last.

A white trailer is at the end of one narrow lane near a collection of tents, with lettering on the side in both English and Arabic that says "Hands and Hearts for Syria." There's a white canvas tarp hanging over the rear of the trailer, where a tired-looking man in khaki pants and a white T-shirt washes his hands under a dribbling faucet. He's wearing wire-rimmed glasses and he's bald, save for a frizzy fringe of white hair that circles his bare head.

I step under the tarp and say, "Spare a prayer, Padre?"

He looks up, startled. Peter "Padre" Picard, former US Army

Ranger, is a good guy to have at your back during a firefight or a bar brawl. He looks at me and says, "The day I say a prayer over you, Mister Taylor, a bolt of lightning will smoke your ass."

He takes off his glasses, wipes the lenses with his T-shirt, puts them back on. Then he says, "What brings you to this newest circle of hell, Dante?"

"On a job."

"I see. Want a drink?"

"What do you have?"

"Right now, warm bottled water or cold bottled water."

"Second sounds great."

He steps into the trailer, comes back out and hands me a plastic bottle. We sit down at the picnic table and we both take long swallows. I say, "How long have you been here?"

"Six months that feels like six years."

"Doing any good?"

"Lots," he says, "though truth be told, sometimes I feel like I'm shoveling against the goddamn tide, the tide being ignorance, tribes, disease, and Russian-made weapons from land mines to AK-47s."

"Then why stick around?"

He shrugs, takes another swig from the plastic bottle. "A number of reasons. Me and my little group, we do make a difference. You can look back and say you saved that kid from cholera, saved that family from starving, saved that teen girl from being raped. Little victories. But to tell you the truth, I'm here to atone for my sins."

"Padre . . ."

"Let me finish, you heathen," he says with a tired smile. "I look back on what I've done in this world, and at the end of the day, it's dead bodies. That's all."

"For a purpose, for a mission."

He peers at me and says, "That's where we're different, old friend. You lean toward black and white, I lean toward shades of gray. Nothing wrong with that, that's how we're wired. But that's why I'm here. To make penance." I swallow some more water and he goes on. "Now you know my sad story. What's yours? What's your job?"

"I'm looking for Jack Zach," I say. "I hear he's in this camp."

Pete laughs. "Yeah. He was. For three days. But he's gone now."

Damn.

"Did he go back to the States?"

"No idea," he says.

Damn again.

I hear the honk of horns, the many scared voices, smell of fire and trash. I can't even see the sky with all the white canvas around us.

"Well, maybe he did good," I say. "Coming here and doing a story about your camp. Show the world what's really going on."

Padre laughs so hard he has to take off his glasses to wipe his eyes. When he's done, he says, "Sure, old Jack Zach did a story here . . . He was with a group of European lingerie models who were doing a charity stunt. Jack got a lot of footage of them tossing out boxes of meals, and bending over to show off their butts and cleavage. Care to guess what got the most attention from Jack Zach?"

# CHAPTER 15

**LATER SOME OF** Padre's staff comes dribbling in and there's conversation in Turkish, English, and French. The fire is at full roar and there's a dinner of rice, flatbread, spicy kebab, and hummus. I sit at the picnic table with Padre and we laugh and talk some, but there's no talk of our past. It would seem out of place here, in this place of rescue and healing.

I feel tired, jet-lagged, and discouraged, but when I help wash the dinner dishes and metal pots, that all changes.

"Hey mister?" a young man asks. He's twenty or so, wearing gray sweatpants, dirty sneakers, and a New York Yankees T-shirt. He's standing next to me and is vigorously drying the dishes with a dirty cotton towel.

"Yeah, what's up?" I ask. He's slim, with dark eyes, wispy beard, thick black hair.

"My name is Yusuf," he says. "I hear you talking about Jack, the camera reporter from America?"

I stop washing and wipe my hands on a spare towel. "Go on."

"I know where he is." He smiles. "You pay me, I take you to him. You see, Jack Zach, he went across the border . . . He's in Syria now.

Doing a bang-bang story." He slaps his chest. "You pay me, I take you to him."

"Can you prove it?" I ask. "That you know where he is? That you know Jack Zach?"

A hand dives into a baggy pocket of his sweatpants, comes out with a photograph of the one and only.

With his still-damp fingers, Yusuf points out a scrawl that I can make out in the light of the fire:

*To my friend Yusuf, all best, Jack Zach.*

I give him his photograph back.

"You have a deal."

Two hours later, I'm with Yusuf and an older man who says he's Nazim, his cousin, and we're walking on a rocky trail to the south of the refugee camp. Yusuf and Nazim are both carrying AK-47s and web belting, and I'm making do with my SIG Sauer and a Kevlar vest.

Other armed men are out there in small groups. We ignore them and they ignore us. The place is littered with white trash bags and mounds of crumpled shipping containers. We approach a chain-link fence. A large gap has been cut in one section, and we each go in. Yusuf whispers to me, "Welcome to Syria."

"Thanks."

"Jack Zach," he whispers. "Not too far away. He . . . how you say? He is playing at being deep in Syria with the bad men . . . But he's really at a tent site . . . relaxing . . . a quick walk away."

I say, "Sounds good to me."

Nazim—who has a thick mustache and blank eyes that reveal nothing—says, "You stay with us. You stay on trail. Go off trail . . . *boom!* Land mines. Very bad."

"Agreed," I say, remembering land mines from my past. "Very bad."

The way is mostly rocks, grass, and scrub brush, and the lights of the camp are bright and bold. I make note of little landmarks as we move along: the pile of broken bottles, the discarded RPG launcher, the clump of white plastic bags stuck in some brush. Other trails go off to the left and right, and way off to the west, there's the rattle of automatic weapons fire. I can see orange tracers dance in long flickering lines. A familiar sight but not a familiar place. I'm all alone, not working with a multibillion-dollar defense agency behind me, and I'm only thinking about the shattered friend of mine who had been betrayed, the one who's now lying in a bed in Georgia.

Yesterday I was in Manhattan and now I'm in barren territory that's been bloodied over the centuries by the Greeks, Romans, Arabs, Turks, Kurds, and now—

Nazim speaks sharply to Yusuf, and they turn to me, AK-47s pointed in my direction and at a trail intersection marked with piles of stone.

Yusuf says, "Sorry, mister. Don't move."

# CHAPTER 16

**BUT I DO** move and instantly drop and roll—as if I had suddenly caught fire—as Yusuf and Nazim shout with surprise and pull the triggers on their automatic rifles. There's the familiar stuttering roar of 7.62mm rounds as bullets zip over my head.

I don't know what the hell is driving them but that's for me to contemplate later. I take a breath, wait, and they fire again. I recognize Nazim as the bigger threat, so when he's lit up by the flash from his AK-47, I quickly fire off two rounds from my SIG Sauer, dropping him hard to the ground.

I roll again, keeping head and vital body parts down. Yusuf starts wailing and fires off another burst.

There are two logical options available to me. I could wait for another burst of fire from the young man and put him down to join his cousin. Or I could crawl away and follow my landmarks to make my way back to the fence and into Turkey.

But when have I ever been logical?

I move quietly, circling around to the other side of Yusuf. He's yelling at me in Arabic and fires off another long burst—fire discipline is definitely not his strong suit—and when he empties his magazine and struggles to replace it, I get up and run at him and roll him over like an NFL player angry at the world.

His AK-47 goes flying off and he hits the dirt hard. I throttle him for a moment, then grab a handful of his greasy hair and slam his head hard against the rocky ground.

Once I have his attention, I say in a loud whisper, "What the hell was that about?"

He's bawling and speaking Arabic, so I slap his face twice and say, "English. What just happened?"

"You . . . you . . . you killed my cousin!" he yells.

"Keep your damn voice down!"

He says, "Nazim . . . you killed my cousin . . ."

"Yeah, well, you guys shot first. Was this a robbery? Or a ransom?"

"I can't tell you, mister . . ."

Not a very proud moment but I have to keep at it. I could have killed him or safely retreated, but by doing so, I wouldn't have gotten what I wanted: intel. Were these two just trying to rob me or hold me hostage?

Or something else?

I throttle Yusef again until he almost passes out, give him one more head slam, and then he says, "Please . . . stop . . ."

"What was the deal, then?"

"Nazim . . . poor Nazim . . ."

"It's going to be poor Yusuf in about ten seconds."

I give the area a quick glance. I can sense movement out there, shadows moving here to the site of the gunfire eruption.

"I . . . we . . . we were told to take you to the meeting place . . . that trail junction . . . and to wait for others to get you . . ."

"Who others?"

"Nazim . . . he knew . . ."

"Why? Ransom? Something else?"

"I . . . was told to talk to you . . . The man who was looking for Jack Zach . . ."

I make out a knot of men at the trail juncture, the one marked with rocks, and decide it's time to bug out. I grab his arm and say, "Move . . . and keep down."

I half drag Yusuf along with me and as we head back to the border fence say, "Who talked to you about me? Who was it?"

"Some . . . American . . ."

"What was his name? Where did you meet?"

"He was a big man, wide and—"

A burst of automatic gunfire and I drop to the ground. Yusuf pulls free and he starts running away, holding up his hands. There's another stutter of gunfire and Yusef runs off the trail. There's a sudden *thump!* of an explosion as he trips over a land mine and pieces of him go windmilling into the air.

# CHAPTER 17

**I'M HOPING THE** sudden noise of the explosion will shock my pursuers for a few seconds, since I'll take any additional second I can get.

I stay as low as I can but I trot quickly along the stone trail, checking off the landmarks as I get closer to the fence.

There's an occasional shot back there, but no muzzle flash.

Swell. That means they're a step up in professionalism from the poorly departed cousins, because they use flash-suppressors to help hide their locations and carefully fire their shots without standing up and spraying the landscape.

I pause, roll, and take cover by a collection of head-sized stones.

Which seems swell, part two. I can only see flickering shadows back here, but as I approach the fence, I realize I'm now backlit by the refugee camp's bright lights.

Like a moving target that can't be missed.

From my place of concealment, I fire off twice—hoping the rocks will block the flash of light from my SIG Sauer—and keep on moving, moving, moving.

I eye the fence line . . . if I can pass through that, at least I'll be back in Turkey. Not meaning I'll be safe, but at least I know one friendly face.

I pause once more, my breathing sharp and hard, and take another two shots at my pursuers.

They fire back, rounds whizzing overhead, one snapping at a near rock.

They're good.

Not very good, but good enough.

I keep on moving.

There's the fence line, up ahead, the place where the gap had been cut open.

And it's blocked.

By three, maybe four shapes, holding AK-47s.

Okay.

Blocked at the rear, blocked at the front.

Land mines out there somewhere.

I throw myself down flat on the dry ground and look back.

Shadows move in my direction and get more distinct as they come closer to me.

I hear a voice, speaking accented but clear English: "Give it up. You can't move."

I keep my mouth shut.

The pursuers get closer.

The shadows out there by the fenceline get more distinct.

Three men block my approach.

My SIG Sauer has a twenty-round magazine, and I have fourteen shots left.

Better be enough.

Because I have no intention of staying here and being captured. I don't want to become the latest hostage who's kept for years before being beheaded or burnt alive.

I stand up and start running to the fence and to Turkey, shooting as fast as I can pull the trigger.

# CHAPTER 18

**RUNNING TO THE** fence isn't as suicidal as it sounds. First, the three men are backlit—just like me—and they make easy targets. While I was running full-bore at them, I fired and moved in zigzags, making me a hard target to hit. Second, these gents made a classic mistake: because they blocked me fore and aft in straight lines, they set it up so they couldn't quickly fire without hitting their friends.

The three shapes collapse and I keep on firing, to make sure they're down for good and not faking it. My pistol's slide slams back and stays in position—indicating I'm out of ammo—and I push the magazine release, popping out the empty, and I grab a full magazine from a pouch at my side, and—

Instantly drop it.

Moron.

I turn and reach to the ground, waiting to be slammed or hit, wounded or killed. When I pick up my magazine, slide it into the pistol grip, and free the slide, I'm thinking I'm one lucky son of a bitch, because . . .

Nobody's following me.

What?

I turn to the fence line and the opening, and beyond there, I see little flickers of light, like fireflies, and a whispering noise going past me.

I move past the crumpled shapes on the ground and carefully step through the cut-out fence, now back in Turkey, and a familiar voice calls out: "That you, heathen?"

I holster my SIG Sauer. "That's right, Padre."

I go farther into Turkey and Peter emerges from the darkness, by a waist-high pile of trash and broken boxes near the crumpled shipping containers, dressed as before, except he has on a Kevlar vest, identical to mine.

"You all right?" he asks.

"Doing fine, except there are some bad guys chasing me."

"No more," he says.

"For real?"

He turns and says, "Aza! We're clear over here."

Another man steps from the shadows, small and bulky looking, holding a rifle that's complete with night vision scope and sound suppressor at the end of the long barrel. He has on a black baseball cap, brim at the rear, a checked black and white scarf, and dark pants and shirt. He's late thirties, with a fierce-looking Fu Manchu mustache, and he nods.

He fades back into the darkness and I say, "Pretty brave, being an armed Kurd here in Turkey."

Peter nods and says, "Aza is here because, a few years back, when I was stationed in Kurdistan . . . well, I did his father a service. So now Aza's my permanent bodyguard and looks out for me in other ways. Like covering a friend who's hauling ass with a squad of bad guys chasing him."

"I didn't see him when I arrived or when I left."

"Pretty good at his job, eh?"

Back at Peter's trailer he says, "What the hell was that all about? You did a crappy job, sliding out with Aza picking you up so easily."

"You knew I was crossing the border?"

"Yusuf's a good worker, but he also has a smuggling sideshow going on over in Syria. I didn't think he was going to give you a tour of the camp."

"So you and Aza were waiting at the crossing, making sure I was covered if need be."

"Good thing I was," he says. "I may be atoning for my sins, but I sure as hell ain't no pacifist who leaves old friends hanging. And why were you so intent on getting across the border anyway?"

"Yusuf told me that Jack Zach was over there."

"You believed him?"

"Enough to go with him."

He turns and looks back into the darkness of Syria. "Where's Yusuf?"

"Tried to run away from me through a mine field. Didn't work out for him."

Peter says, "Jesus, you can't stay away from trouble, can you?"

"Apparently not."

Inside the trailer it's dark and crowded, with cardboard boxes and mismatched chairs. Peter shuffles around and comes back with two cold bottles of Efes Pilsen and opens them both. I take a long, refreshing slug and he says, "You looking for Jack Zach . . . A private job?"

"Yes."

"Pays well?"

"Not a damn dime."

"That's the Owen I know," he says. "What do you need now?"

"I need to get back to the airport at Gaziantep, preferably with my head intact."

Peter smiles. "Demanding cuss, aren't you?"

"Like you said, you know me well."

# CHAPTER 19

**AFTER SPENDING LESS** than a day in Turkey and Syria, I'm retracing my steps, thinking of my time there and what happened to me. I'm getting the feeling that Yusuf, Nazim, and the other gunmen were not only up to no good, but that they had somebody with money and authority employing them.

But for what reason? To get me? Lots of opportunities for bad folks over the years to get me, and nothing ever happened. So why now?

To protect Jack Zach?

If so, who's doing the protecting? His new Taliban buddies? Not likely. They're thousands of klicks away and they usually have problems doing anything outside of their provinces. They don't have the reach.

Is Jack Zach protecting himself?

Not by hiring losers like Yusuf or Nazim. He'd hire better losers with polished shoes and nice suits and law offices in downtown Manhattan.

There are lots of things to think about, but for now I'm relaxing in the first class section of an Air France Boeing 777, heading back to

JFK. I've paid a good chunk of cash to upgrade myself, and considering that desperate and dirty time back in Syria, I think it's money well spent. Each seat is a little luxurious space pod with a television screen, and dinner somewhere over the Atlantic includes tournedos and a choice of five different wines.

I sleep, and before I know it, we descend and land with a soft whisper. In minutes, we roll up to Terminal 1. With my false identification, I get through Customs.

And there you go. Allison is waiting for me on the other side, and I'm pretty sure it's not a good sign. She has on her uniform of black blazer, white blouse, black slacks, and black heels. It sounds plain but still, she looks pretty damn good.

Allison comes up to me and says, "We have a problem."

All right, I'm certain it's not a good sign.

"What's up?"

She motions me to follow her and we find a quiet corner. The terminal has lots of big white tubes and trusses overhead, like some crazed architect's idea of what the future would look like in the go-go 1980s.

Allison says, "We need to get down to Georgia."

"But will the devil beat us there?"

She swears at me with the grace and accomplishment of one so long working in the shadows of the government service, and says, "Cut it out. You got everything you need?"

I hold up my carry-on. "Right here."

"Then let's haul ass. We got a flight leaving in thirty-five minutes to Atlanta, and we're in the wrong terminal."

She starts walking at a fast clip and I keep right up with her.

I ask, "What's the trouble?"

"I'll brief you on the drive out of Atlanta. No one can listen in then." She takes a glance at my unshaven face and slept-in clothes. "How was Turkey?"

"Turkey was fine, save for a brief and violent excursion into Syria."

"What happened?"

I smile at her. "I'll brief you on the drive out of Atlanta."

# CHAPTER 20

**WE CRASH IN** an airport hotel, and the next morning make the hour drive to Barnes. After our promised mutual briefing, we roll back in front of the nice home in the nice neighborhood of the nice town of Barnes, Georgia. Right away, I sense that something is off.

The landscape and the road and the kids playing around are the same, but there are two young men working on the porch of Ray and Marilyn's house.

We wait for a minute in the car. "That's where it happened?" I ask.

"That's right," she says. "At about the same time you were spreading peace, love, and understanding in Syria."

"Interesting timing," I say.

"Let's go."

Outside the air smells much more refreshing than it did in Turkey, without thousands of desperate people clustered around in trailers and white tents.

I say, "You know how we travelers would sometimes stop and ask each other, 'Hey, what day is it?' I feel like you need to tell me what month it is."

"Whatever month it is, it's a month of problems," Allison says.

We get up to the porch and the workers ignore us, but I can't ignore what's resting against the porch railing: the original door to the house, with its center shattered and blasted out. There's also a peppering of shotgun pellets in a pattern around the opening, and I note the scent of burnt gunpowder.

The two workers have unpacked a new door from a cardboard covering, and we pass them as we walk into the entryway and the converted parlor. A temporary green cloth screen on casters is shielding most of the hospital bed, and there's a chubby male medical aide assisting Ray, whose good eye is closed. I spend a second looking at the bare flesh, the sutured skin, the burn tissue and bandaged stumps, and I look away.

There's something new in the room, leaning against the near wall: a Mossberg Model 500 .20-gauge pump-action shotgun.

Marilyn comes in from the other room, anger coming off her approach and eyes. She has on khaki slacks and a red turtleneck shirt that's sleeveless, and says, "About time you two clowns showed up."

Allison says, "We got here as quick as we could. Give us the whole story."

"Ever since you two noble folks left, Raynie and I have been harassed. Late night doorbell ringing, hang-up phone calls, two broken windows. Then somebody slipped this flyer under the front door."

Ray cries out and the medical aide says something soothing, and there's a sob and silence. Marilyn clenches her jaw and goes over to a bookcase, where she picks up a folded sheet of white paper. She passes it over and Allison opens it. I read it next to her:

BACK OFF. EVEN BRAVE VETS CAN DIE
BY ACCIDENT.

It's printed in a plain black sans-serif font from an inkjet printer, practically impossible to trace.

Allison passes the paper back to Marilyn and she crumples it up and throws it on the floor. I ask, "So what did you do?"

Marilyn says, "I put a nice bag of stinking trash out there, where they delivered the note, hoping they'd get the signal."

I try not to smile. I'm a little scared of this woman. "What happened next?"

"Last night, I thought I heard somebody on the porch. I went around to the side window, saw two men. They were bent over, like they were trying to break in."

"Did you warn them?" Allison asked.

"Fire first, questions later, Raynie always told me," Marilyn says with steel in her voice. "I grabbed the shotgun from the rear closet, blasted right at them."

Another soft moan comes from behind the curtain. Allison glances at me and then to Marilyn. "We . . . can stop, if you want. That's not a problem. If you have any regrets."

Marilyn crosses her arms, snaps off a fierce nod. "Regrets? I have two regrets. One, I woke up Raynie . . . and he was sleeping good that night. Second . . . that there weren't any bloodstains on the porch when I checked it out. That means I missed."

I hear soft whispers again from the medical aide.

Marilyn says, "Jack Zach? You destroy that man."

# CHAPTER 21

**ON THE WAY** back to Atlanta on I-20, Allison is still driving, which I think is a grand idea, for I'm going to raise a subject that's going to test her and test us. If she's occupied with driving, I'm hoping that it'll work in my favor.

"Got a moment?" I ask.

She checks the rental vehicle's dashboard clock. "If the traffic doesn't get any heavier, you've got lots of moments. What's up?"

I peek at the side-view mirror. There's a Chevy Suburban a ways behind us, weaving through traffic.

I say, "Why are you here?"

"Pretty apparent," she says. "I'm driving us to the airport."

"Stop playing around." I look to the side-view mirror, noticing that the Suburban is definitely approaching us.

"You know me by now, I don't play."

"Maybe, maybe not. Still not sure what you do on your off hours . . . if you have them. But there are hundreds—if not thousands—of guys like Ray Winston, all across the country. Why are you standing up for him? Why are you jeopardizing your career over one disabled soldier?"

I think she wants to strike out with her hand and slap me one, but I'm over as far as I can be on the passenger's side. I go on. "So it's Ray Winston, here in Georgia. Injured because Jack Zach was a creep who wanted a story, and the Taliban gave him one. But he's also injured because of what Marilyn said, that first day. Ray and his unit weren't supposed to go out that night. But they were ordered to do so. By you . . . right?"

Now I think Allison wants to ram the rental into the nearest bridge abutment, and I say, "High value target nearby? Somebody you wanted to kill or capture that was worth the risk?"

She says, "Yeah."

"What kind of high value target?"

"The kind of target that has a high value on it, and that later turns out not to be there," she says crisply. "Meaning some good soldiers got slaughtered and shattered for nothing."

I think of my friend Pete Picard, over there in Turkey. "Seeking atonement, then."

"Seeking the ability to sleep at night," she says.

I look again at the side-view mirror. Allison slowly changes lanes, and the Suburban stays with us. "Speaking of abilities . . ."

"Yeah, the Suburban back there," she says. "It's been dogging us for the last ten minutes."

"Good eye," I say. "I've only been seeing it for eight. What do you want to do?"

"We have a known unknown back there," she says. "I hate having anything unknown following me."

A sign up ahead says REST AREA ONE MILE.

"Then let's get things known," I say.

In less than sixty seconds, we pull off the highway and come up to a pretty one-story brick building with a green metal roof. It looks like some sort of out-of-the-way chapel for an obscure Christian sect. Allison pulls in and we both get out, and head to our respective rest areas. When I'm done, she isn't in the small lobby, which is okay.

I step outside into the warm Georgia winter sun, and the Chevy Suburban is parked next to our rental car.

Still no Allison.

Definitely not okay.

The right rear door of the Suburban opens. Inside there's a squat, bulky bald man wearing an expensive and well-tailored black pin-striped two-piece suit with white shirt and dark-red tie. He blinks and says, "Mister Taylor, if you please, I'd like a word with you."

I say, "I'd rather wait for my driving companion to come back."

He says, "I'm afraid she's been . . . detained."

The bright Georgia sun seems to kick it up a notch, and I'm sweating even though it's chilly outside. "I know you want to talk to me. I'm not sure if I want to talk to you."

He says, "Want to keep that pretty face on your lady friend? That'll depend on your cooperation. Do I have it?"

I start climbing into the backseat of the Suburban. "You have me," I say.

# CHAPTER 22

**INSIDE THE CLEAN** and tidy interior of the Suburban, it smells of cologne, and I can't tell if it's coming from my Daddy Warbucks companion or his driver. The man in the driver's seat is quiet but built and dressed like the man I'm sitting with, save his head of thick, close-cropped black hair. He backs out and in a few seconds, we're heading east again on I-20.

Supposedly in negotiations, whoever speaks first loses. I don't have anything to say, so I figure that I might as well keep my mouth shut. We drive along until we get to an exit, and then we drive for another ten or so minutes along back roads. We go down an unmarked dirt road and the driver seems sure of where he's going.

The road opens up in a wide spot of grass, about knee-high, and there's a rocky cliff across the way, which looks like it has a stone quarry in the center. I can't see how deep it is from where I'm sitting, but based on these two muscular guys, I guess it will be plenty deep enough to hide whatever they want to hide.

The driver maneuvers around until the Suburban is facing back up the dirt road. He puts it in Park and switches off the engine. The man next to me sighs and says, "The name is Pope."

"How's it going?"

"Lousy," he says. "I had a number of items on my agenda today, and you and your woman friend weren't supposed to be one of them."

"I'd say I'm sorry, but you probably know I'm not."

"True," he says. He shifts in his seat and says, "Your pistol, please. And do me the favor of removing it slowly, and using only the first two fingers of your left hand."

"All right," I say, and the driver has moved around so he's covering me with whatever he had in his lap—which is blocked by the driver's seat—and I helpfully say, "Moving now."

I lean forward and remove my SIG Sauer from my waist holster, and hold it up with the requested two fingers.

Pope says, "Kindly pass it over to Trevor."

I move my gun forward and the driver takes it out of my hand.

Pope sighs. "Very well," he says. "You're starting off reasonable. I like reasonable."

"Don't we all."

Pope says, "You and your friend have been disturbing a delicate balance. We want it to stop."

"Who's 'we'?" I ask. "Members of the Jack Zach fan club? No offense to you and your driver, but I expected that kind of group to trend toward the female audience."

"There's no need for you to know who hired us," he says. "For now, we want you to stop. Do I have your agreement?"

"Nope."

"Why not?"

"Because I'd rather not," I say, starting to brace myself for what's probably going to happen next.

Another sigh from Pope. From a net storage bag in the seat in front of him, he takes out two black leather gloves, and from the way he handles them, I know there's more than just leather there.

He carefully and with precision puts on the lead-lined gloves, and says, "Please forgive me for what I'm about to do, but if you want your female friend to remain unharmed, you'll just have to suck it up."

And then his fist smashes into my face.

# CHAPTER 23

**WHAT HAPPENS NEXT** has been pre-determined from the moment I got into the Suburban back at the rest area. Pope is beating me in a way that causes me the most pain and hurt with only a few well-directed punches that he slams out without exhausting himself. I'm playing the part of the victim, holding up my hands, cowering, crying out with pain and discomfort. I'd be a hard-assed stoic but for a professional like Pope—and in his manner and language, I know he's a professional— that would just lengthen the process for the two of us. He might have a suspicion that I'm overreacting, just to get things done, but as a professional, he'll punish me enough to meet his own personal goals.

But even though a part of me is coldly and rationally analyzing the beating he's giving me, most of all, it hurts like hell.

Long minutes pass, and there's a pause before he resumes.

I grit my teeth, tasting that coppery taste of blood.

At times like this, I hate professionals.

Then he stops, breathing just a bit harder, and says, "I'm sorry for my atavistic nature. But I do find it gets me in the mood to have an open and frank exchange of views."

The driver passes over a white handkerchief. Pope wipes the gloves as best as he can, removes them, and delicately passes everything back to his driver.

"Then get on with it," I say, feeling the puffiness in my lips.

"You've been after Jack Zach. Stop it."

"Why?"

His right hand moves as fast as a rattlesnake strike, punching my very sore face. I gasp out something and fall back against the door.

"Isn't that a good enough reason?" he asks. "Or should I ask Trevor to return the gloves to me?"

My mouth is full with saliva and blood, and I lean forward and let it drip out onto the floor. I wipe at my lips and say, "Maybe. But why don't you humor me. You seem to be in a good mood."

Pope shakes his head for a moment, like he can't believe he has to put up with my attitude. "Jack Zach is a fool, a headline grabber, and a hack that would sell his soul—if he had one—to get a scoop, a story, anything that would put his name out there. Then, like a gambler who needs another high, he rests for a moment before going out again."

"That's no surprise."

I move slowly, rubbing at my sore face and trying to gauge the damage.

As I wince in pain, something comes to me. I say, "You been to Turkey lately?"

The slight smile tells me all I need to know. Pope doesn't answer, and instead says, "You'll back off?"

"Hard to do so right now," I say.

Pope says, "Don't be surprised at the depth of his protection. We won't allow you to threaten him."

# CHAPTER 24

**THERE'S A FLICKER** of light and shadows, and another black Chevy Suburban is coming down the dirt road. Pope says, "Your companion is in that vehicle. I'm sure you're aware of how remote it is around here, and that you and your friend are outnumbered."

"Well, I've been pretty distracted these past few minutes, but I see what you mean."

"Do you?"

The other Suburban makes a wide turn, backs in so that it's parallel to the one we're in. Like the Chevy I'm in, it also has tinted windows.

Pope shifts some, his weight making the seat creak. "Then let me make it very, very clear. This is your last chance to make your intentions known."

I say, "Remind me again what you're looking for?"

His lips purse. "You will cease all activities with regards to Jack Zach. You will step away, you will halt, you will even refrain from mentioning Jack Zach in polite company. Do I make myself clear?"

"Very," I say. "But you forgot one important matter. You didn't say, 'or else.' Isn't that part of the routine?"

"You think I have a routine?"

"Pope, you've got something, I'll give you that."

"What you did have was time, and you're now out of time. You say what I want to hear, or the treatment I gave you will be considered a spa session compared to what we have in store for your female friend. Do I have your agreement?"

The driver's side door to the Suburban opens.

Allison steps out.

She's holding a 9mm pistol in her right hand.

I say, "I think my female friend wants to propose another agreement."

Pope shouts to Trevor and with the two of them distracted, I move quickly, reaching into my pocket, pulling out the pen Allison gave me back in New York, and I click the top. But instead of a ballpoint tip, a thin stiletto blade made of carbon steel pops out.

I nail Trevor in the back of his neck, and he squeals loudly, like a little boy stubbing his toe on a rock, and I tug out the stiletto, whirl and stab Pope in the throat. He gurgles and his eyes widen in shock, and one stab was probably enough, but I'm pissed enough at him that I let emotions take over and stab him again.

After retrieving my SIG Sauer from the front seat—and Trevor has both hands on the back of his neck and is crying as he slowly collapses— I get out and Allison says, "Christ, he really beat the crap out of you."

I say, "But he never got my secret chicken recipe."

She looks past me, into the car, and says, "Let's get the hell out of here."

"Agreed."

We go back to the Suburban and for the first time I spot the dried blood on Allison's hands, and some blood spatter on her neck and on the right side of her face.

She says, "I'm driving. And do me a favor, don't look in the back."

"Why?"

Allison puts her 9mm back into a waist holster, underneath her black blazer.

"Even with a pistol, some guys won't listen to an armed woman," she says. "So I did what I had to do."

# CHAPTER 25

ALLISON DRIVES US out and gets us back on the interstate, and making some illegal U-turns, returns us back to the rest area. We dump the Suburban—the rear seat unviewed by yours truly—at the far end of the lot, away from any possible surveillance cameras. Then we get back into our rental car and back on track.

We drive for a bit and find a gas station, where we each take time getting cleaned up. Allison has the easier time of it, since the blood on her face and hands doesn't belong to her, and I do the best I can with my own wounds.

We end up missing our flight from Atlanta-Hartsfield, but we have good excuses, none of which we share with the nice Delta ticketing woman as she sets us up with new arrangements.

Now I'm sitting in a remote part of Concourse A, and when Allison exits the women's room with her hair rearranged in a tight ponytail, I gently applaud and say, "Jesus, you clean up nicely."

Instead of saying something snappy, Allison seems to blush for a second or two, and says, "All right. We got a couple of hours to kill."

"Bad choice of words."

"What, now you're the grammar police?" she asks.

"I'll show you my badge if you like," I say.

She sits next to me. "From what that guy Pope told you, we're never going to get close to Jack Zach. He's a protected asset, and in troubled times like these, corporations are going to protect things that bring in a steady income stream."

I had made a compress of paper towels and cold water, and now move it from one aching part of my face to the other. "They also have a pretty long reach. Somehow they knew I was in Turkey, looking for their best boy, and then they tried to snatch me in Syria."

"Tricky bastards."

"And powerful bastards," I say. "The company and whatever friends and co-workers he has won't give him up. He probably has a half dozen condos, chalets, and cabins to hide out in, and if we follow him on television, we'll always be a day behind."

"What do you suggest?"

I wiggle my jaw. It seems like all my teeth are still in place. Good.

"We broaden the battlefield," I say. "Look at the backgrounds of some of the network's execs. Or their advertisers. Or staff that work out of their Manhattan office. Somewhere, somehow, someone will crack, or give us a lead."

Allison frowns. "That'll take some time."

"What, you got a bus to catch?"

An odd beeping sound blurts out from somewhere and I look around our seating area, and Allison says, "Hey, big boy, check your pockets. That's your cell phone talking to you."

Sure enough, I pull my cell phone out of my coat pocket and swipe through the screens, and find an incoming text:

PLEASE SEE ME AS SOON AS YOU CAN.

"Well?" Allison demands.

I read her the text and she says, "Where did that come from?"

"Rachel Cooper," I say. "Wife of Jack Zach's favorite cameraman."

One hand holding the phone, I move the compress again. Allison says, "She was pretty adamant that she didn't want to deal with us."

"Something's changed."

"Apparently so, and probably for the better," I say. "Looks like we're going back to New Rochelle."

"Might be a trap," Allison says.

"You and I have been lucky so far."

"No, we haven't," Allison points out. "We've been good."

"But not cocky," I say.

"Never cocky," Allison says.

# CHAPTER 26

**AFTER REPLYING TO** Rachel's text, it's time to board our flight back to JFK. Once again, I pay to upgrade the tickets to first class.

Once we've eaten our meals of pasta and drunk our wine, I ask for a warm towel. Allison looks to me and I say, "You missed a couple of spots on your neck. We don't want Rachel Cooper to think poorly of your grooming skills, especially after a very deadly event."

"How do you know it was a deadly event?" she asks. "Maybe one of my captors had a nosebleed, and I just tried to help."

"Yes, you always have been the helpful one. Lift up your chin, turn right."

Allison does that and I locate two smears of rust-red dried blood at her jawline, just above her slim and delicate neck. I gently rub the dried blood and it comes off. She sighs and seems to enjoy my touch, so I don't pull away. I keep on gently rubbing and rubbing. Her skin is smooth and flawless.

She turns her head and I say, "Believe it or not, it looks like you have a scratch."

"Really?"

"Really."

She gives me a smile that's part mocking, part inviting. "What do you intend to do about it?"

I say, "Kiss it and make it better."

I gently put my right hand around her neck and equally gently pull her to me, and I kiss her cheek, jawline, and her neck. I stay at her neck for delicious seconds, and then move to her lips.

Maybe it's just the sheer pleasure of feeling and tasting her after my days on the run, shooting and being shot at, but the sensation is intoxicating. I draw back for a moment and she puts a finger on my lips and says, "Wait."

"For what?"

A peck to my nose. "You think I missed a couple of spots? You should see your neck. Ask the flight attendant for some more towels. And I'll return the favor."

As we're waiting for the towels, I think: to hell with the rules, to hell with the regulations. If Allison wants to know what happened in Serbia, I'll tell her.

I'll tell her right now.

I turn away from the aisle, toward Allison. "Hey, I want to—"

Then I shut up.

She's curled up, fast asleep.

So as not to annoy her, I take out a book and start to read.

Allison stirs and wakes up at the sound of the Boeing 767's tires striking the pavement of JFK's Runway 4L-22R. She wipes at her eyes.

"We're here," I say.

She yawns and says, "So . . . what happened while I was sleeping?"

"You were ravished and brought to levels of ecstasy not known to ordinary women."

She yawns again. "And yet I slept right through it. Poor me."

The aircraft starts taxiing and she says, "Owen . . . no offense, but it's mission first, all right?"

I squeeze her hand and she squeezes back. So at least there's that.

"Mission first," I say.

# CHAPTER 27

**BACK IN NEW** Rochelle and the pleasant suburban home of Walt and Rachel Cooper, there's a sense that something wrong has happened, of some untold foul doing. The place looks the same and Rachel tries to be cheerful and welcoming, but she's failing.

Her eyes are swollen, like she's been crying a lot, or staring back at something that has happened and not liking the way it looks. She has on jeans and a shapeless gray sweatshirt with a NY Giants emblem on the front, and she leads us through the living room, where two young girls are on the couch, watching some animated movie on television.

Rachel says, "Stacy? Anna? I'll be upstairs for a while with our guests. Keep it down, okay?"

The girls murmur something and keep focused on the dancing dragons on television. Allison and I go upstairs and Rachel leads us left, to the master bedroom. She sits on the edge of the bed and says, "This won't take long."

Allison says, "We'll give you as much time as you like."

She nods and she bites her lower lip, and she looks like she's going to burst into tears, but she swallows and says, "Jack Zach was here earlier."

I keep quiet. So does Allison.

Then I finally ask, "Where's your husband?"

"In Jordan, filming B-roll of refugee camps."

Allison says, "All right."

Rachel takes a deep sigh, pulls a piece of clothing from underneath the bed covering. It's a black silk blouse, and it's torn. Rachel crumples it up in her hands and puts them in her lap.

"He . . . he said that if I didn't cooperate, he could make things very, very bad for my husband."

"Doesn't your husband work for the network?" I ask. "Aren't there . . . protections?"

"No," Rachel says. "Walt's an independent contractor, working for Jack Zach's production company. He's on his own."

I want to say something but Allison nudges me with her hip. "So much for loyalty," she says.

Rachel says, "So much."

She drops the ruined blouse on the floor. "You two . . . why do you want to see Jack Zach so badly?"

Allison says, "He severely hurt a friend of ours, and killed others close to that friend."

"So . . . something bad will happen to Jack Zach if you meet him?"

I say, "That's the plan."

Rachel drops the blouse and kicks it under the bed, hiding it from view. "Then I'm going to give the two of you a tip. There's a get-together tomorrow night, at an exclusive restaurant in Manhattan. Jack hosts it every year. You want to get to Jack? You go there." She scribbles down the information on a piece of paper.

I take the paper, and Allison and I get up to leave.

And right before we reach the door, we hear Rachel's voice again. "Oh, and when you see him?"

I turn around to listen carefully.

"I want you to hurt him. Hurt him bad."

"We're on it," I say.

# CHAPTER 28

**THE NEXT NIGHT,** I'm back with Allison in a black GMC Yukon, parked illegally on Seventh Avenue, in front of a row of office buildings and high-priced shops, including one place that has a double glass door—darkened—with a simple pink neon sign above that says JEAN-PAUL.

Allison says, "This place is so exclusive that you have to give them your name, your background, and credit report, and then they call you to extend an invitation."

"I thought Jack Zach said he was a man of the people."

"He is," Allison says. "He just doesn't say what kind of people."

Like the last time we were in Manhattan, the weather is wet and overcast, but it's dark out, meaning I can't see anything of the upper floors of the buildings. Traffic flows past, and umbrella-covered pedestrians trudge by.

Allison checks the time. "Our boy should be in there, working on his second martini and his first married woman of the night."

A blare of horns and a taxi cab zips by, nearly running down a couple. I say, "Hey, about our flight to JFK . . ."

"Mission first, remember?"

"Oh, I remember," I say. "But on the flight back, I wanted to talk to you about something."

"What?"

"My last op."

She stares at me. "Now? Now you're ready to be noble and give it up? Why?"

"Because . . . because I want to. To hell with the rules."

"What a bad boy you are." And then comes the big surprise of the evening when she says, "But don't."

"Excuse me?" I ask. "Twice before you've pushed me, and twice before I've pushed you back. Now I'm ready to roll over and present up my belly like a goofy Labrador retriever, and you're saying no?"

"That's right," she says. "It's not the time. Mission first, Owen. Go out there and do your job. You ready?"

"I am."

"Good."

No time for debate or discussion.

She's right.

I open the Yukon's door and step outside into the darkness and rain.

# CHAPTER 29

**AS I ENTER** the luxurious and glamorous world of the restaurant called Jean-Paul, I remember sitting under a Georgia pine tree, eating a cold MRE of pork and beans, while a special operations instructor repeated the most important word in certain missions: *confidence, confidence, confidence.*

"If you can show you're confident and that you belong there, you can walk through Grand Central Terminal wearing just a jock strap, and no one will blink an eye," he said.

Well, I'm dressed in my nice suit and I have a big smile as I walk in, come right up against the maître d' station, and I nod and whisper, "I'm from INN and need to see Jack Zach." The maître d' is a silver-haired man dressed in a crisp evening suit. He says, "Please, sir, can you wait . . ." as I confidently stride right past him.

I go through a small but comfortable dining room with tiny tables, white tablecloths, and well-dressed people. I recognize a competing news anchor and two NBA players. Moving with confidence, I know exactly where I'm going, thanks to some quick, dark work on Allison's part, who had given me a floor schematic of Jean-Paul.

Striding down an unmarked hallway, I pass rows of shelving

containing wine bottles. I open an oak door and go right into Jack Zach's private room. It's wood paneled and decorated with small oil paintings done in the Hudson River style of the mid-1800s.

"Jack!" I call out, stepping up to his table. It's rectangular and covered with a white cloth, with Jack sitting at the head—which is to my left—and there are seven other diners there, four women, three men. I instantly note the two men sitting at my right, on either side of the table. The muscle. They're dressed well but they don't look comfortable in their suits, like trained Doberman pinschers being forced to wear a ballet skirt for a photo shoot. The three women are in their early twenties, dressed spectacularly in varying degrees of exposed skin, and the other man is older, perhaps Jack's attorney or business manager.

There are open wine bottles on the table, and Jack is grinning at me, his hair and beard carefully coifed and trimmed. He's wearing a dark-blue suit with a white turtleneck, looking like some retro-hip Hollywood director from the 1960s.

He says, "You must be that thick man who's intent on meeting me. Sorry, I don't have anything with me to sign."

The women and the older man laugh, but the muscles stay silent.

I say, "Jack, it's time for you to make amends."

Jack says, "What? Are you going to shoot me here, in front of all these witnesses?"

No more laughter. Just quiet looks among his guests, and very sharp looks from his two bodyguards, whose right hands have slipped inside their suit jackets.

I stand still, and then move two steps to the right, to the near bodyguard.

"Jack . . . you know, you're right. I'm sorry to interrupt your evening, and your meal." I slowly start moving to my right. "I really just wanted to meet you so bad, Jack, I see you on TV all the time and it's not often I get to meet someone famous!"

Then, with no warning, I punch the nearest bodyguard in the back of the head, knocking him out. Simultaneously, I grab a bottle of wine with my other hand and hurl it at the other guard's head. While he throws his hands up to block it, I run around the table and smash him in the face.

Once.

Twice.

He stops moving.

Chaos.

The young ladies scream and the older man huddles forward, like he's trying to reduce his target signature. I move up the table and Jack starts speaking, and I give him a good slap to the face. Then I grab his right arm and pick him up from his chair.

Overwhelming and sudden force is the key. These people are in an exclusive restaurant—safe, warm, and well fed—and they have no imagination that something bad will happen to them. Even when it does happen—like right now—they can't comprehend, they can't process, can't do a thing.

Like how some determined men with box cutters hijacked jet airliners back in the day.

Jack says, "Hey, hey, hey—"

But I interject and say, "Keep your mouth shut." I twist his right arm up, grab his thumb, and tuck it under his armpit, and I propel him out of the room.

He arches his back and tears are in his eyes. I'm using an old police tool, called a "come-along," which radiates sharp pain through his right arm and shoulder, and makes him do what I want him to do, which is to quickly get out of Jean-Paul.

I go through the main dining room, holding Jack close to me, and the pain radiating in his right arm and shoulder is keeping him under my control. The other diners look up and I can sense their confusion: what's going on? Is Jack being arrested? Is he in trouble?

And most of all: what should we do?

I get past the maître d' station and what I knew would happen happens.

Which is nothing.

In one of the most exclusive restaurants in Manhattan, the scene is over in a few seconds. No one is going to stand up from their table and disturb the meal of a lifetime.

We go outside in the rain, among the pedestrians, and I'm feeling pretty good.

The night is off to a good start.

Then it all goes wrong.

I'm at the edge of the sidewalk, where the Chevy is parked.

But Allison's gone.

And she has the keys.

# CHAPTER 30

**JACK SENSES SOMETHING** is up and through his pain says, "What's the matter, pal? Your ride go missing? You get abandoned?"

I say, "You're no pal."

I start moving him and he emits a sharp groan, and says, "Let me go, right here, and I won't call the cops, won't cause a problem. Christ, it hurts!"

"Shut your mouth, Jack. This is my remote stand-up, not yours."

I move him past the people walking quickly in the rain, glad to see that the typical New York pedestrian habit—eyes down, don't pay attention, not your business—is working in my favor. All it would take would be a passing NYPD cop or building security guard to ruin everything.

Resources.

I need to use available resources.

Cabs are driving by; there's no way I'm going to find an empty taxi in the rain.

What to do?

Resources.

At the corner of Seventh Avenue and West 57th, there's a black

Lexus LS parked illegally, engine running. I open the rear door, push Jack in, get in, and slam the door behind me. A Hispanic man wearing a white shirt and black tie turns from behind the steering wheel and says, "Are you Mister Tremain, my pickup?"

I thrust a fistful of bills over the driver's seat. "Better than that," I say. "I'm Mister Grant and this is Mister Franklin."

The driver smiles as he sees the amount I've passed over to him. "Nice to meet you. Where to?"

"Just start driving. I'll give you the directions and a few more bills," I say.

Now free of my painful grasp, Jack starts to say something, but as the driver is distracted, I grab Jack in a two-hand choke, and carefully count off the seconds—one one-thousand, two one-thousand, three one-thousand, and so on—until he falls unconscious and he's out, hopefully without suffering any brain damage.

The driver looks up to his rearview mirror.

"Everything okay back there?"

I say, "He's just been drinking too much, got too excited."

"He gonna puke?"

"I hope not."

"Me, too," the driver says.

# CHAPTER 31

**THE DRIVER ANSWERS** his cell phone and speaks loudly in Spanish, hangs up and says, "Hey, Mister Tremain, he'll get over it, am I right?"

I pass over two more fifty-dollar bills. "Absolutely."

"Where to, friend?" he asks.

"New Jersey."

"Oh, that's a distance."

A couple more Ben Franklins join the group in our driver's pocket. He chuckles and says, "What the hell, it's been a while since I've taken the tunnel."

I give our driver the directions. Allison had told me it would take about an hour to get there, but probably enthused by the money he's received, our driver gets us there in about fifty minutes, taking the Lincoln Tunnel and then I-95 South. Eventually, we get on Route 24 into northern New Jersey. Along the way Jack murmurs a few times but I give him a twist of the arm to keep him quiet.

The last ten minutes are tricky. We go through some back roads and country lanes, outside of Hanover, and then our driver puts on the high beams in front of a rusty metal gate at the end of an unmarked road.

"That's where the odometer says we should stop," he says. "This the right place?"

"Perfect," I say, passing over one more Ben Franklin. "And to be sure . . . if you're asked what you've been up to the past two hours . . ."

He snaps the bill from my hand. "Couple of Chinese tourists wanted me to take them on a slow-motion tour of Chinatown. Paid in cash. Pretty boring stuff."

"Good."

I open the door and start pulling at Jack, and the driver says, "Hey, I think I know that dude. Isn't he famous?"

"He's nothing," I say. Once we're outside, the Lexus makes a crisp U-turn and is gone.

Jack is gaining confidence as I walk him around the gate and along a gravel path. "What is this . . . a kidnapping? Is that it? Trust me, the network won't pay what you're asking for."

"Oh, I don't know," I say, holding his arm tight, "seems like the network likes you a bunch, the way they've been sticking up for you lately." The way is clear through some trees and high brush, and I hear engines idling not too far away. I check my watch. I should call and see if Allison is all right, but it's going to be tight. Calling her in the livery cab hadn't been an option, either, because I didn't want Jack or our driver to hear what I was saying.

As much as I hate to admit it, I have to leave Allison for later. But I know she can handle herself.

The way in front of us opens up. It's hard to see, but from the ambient night light of New Jersey, I make out a couple of unused buildings to our left. To our right, with its engines idling, is a four-engine Lockheed C-130 Hercules transport aircraft on an old abandoned airstrip. There are only a few lights, but enough to see that the aircraft is painted black and has no markings.

Jack hesitates, and I tug him forward, saying, "Come on, I'm sure an inquisitive war journalist like you would jump at the chance to take a ride on an unregistered secret aircraft. It's all the rage nowadays, to transport naughty folks like you before they disappear."

His feet dig in and it costs me a few seconds, so I do the "come-along" routine again on his right arm. Jack Zach walks on tiptoe as we go to the end of the aircraft, with its rear loading ramp lowered. There are dim red lights inside and the place is empty. We go up the metal ramp and inside there are two rows of red webbed seating, and lots of overhead struts, wires, pipes, and cables.

I push Jack into one of the webbed seats, and fasten his seat belt. Then, just to make sure he's a good boy for the duration of the flight, I fasten some plastic zip ties around his wrists and ankles.

There's a whining noise as the ramp begins to close. I check my watch. Right on time. If I had been sixty seconds late, then this black aircraft would have taken off, leaving me and Jack behind.

The engines roar louder and the aircraft starts moving. I sit across from Jack in my own red webbed seat, and he looks around and his eyes are round and fearful, and if I was in a forgiving mood—which I'm not—I'd feel sorry for him in his blue suit, polished shoes, and white turtleneck as he sits in this mean-looking military aircraft, looking like some frat pledge being taken on the hazing of his life.

I cup my hands around my mouth and yell across at him: "It's not first class with pretty flight attendants, Jack, but it'll do!"

He doesn't say a word, just looks up and down the empty aircraft, as we rise into the New Jersey sky.

# CHAPTER 32

**WHEN THE C-130** reaches what I feel is its cruising altitude, I go forward and find the large zippered black duffel bag that Allison had promised would be waiting for me. I think of trying to text her but a quick glance at my cell phone shows that I have no service. I pull the duffel bag open and take a quick look at the gear.

I take my time surveying the aircraft's interior, and lots of memories come back about traveling in similar aircraft over the years, sometimes on risky missions, sometimes on boring transport lifts from Point A to Point B. Hell, based on the average age of the C-130 airframe in the American military and intelligence agency fleets, there was a good chance I had ridden on this particular plane before.

Lots of those previous flights blur together in my memory, but two of them are crowded in the center of the hull with tied-down aluminum caskets, with American flags carefully tied into place.

Those flights I won't ever forget.

I look to Jack, who is staring back at me in defiance, and I know that chances were very good that the Americans who died under Jack Zach's watch ended up in an aircraft just like this, on their long journey home to the Air Force base in Dover, Delaware.

I have to look down and focus on the book cover, because otherwise I'd go across to the other side of the C-130 and kill him.

I sit still.

Among other things, killing him now would upset my schedule.

Hours later, there's a change in the pitch of the four Rolls-Royce turbo-prop engines, and a couple of ominous sounding *thunks* from the flight cabin. Jack moves against his restraints and his face is pale, and he's yelling something at me, but because of the engine noise, I can't make out a damn word.

I undo my seat belt and carefully walk across to Jack, and I say, "Hey, no worries, Jack. We're doing some mid-air refueling. Up over the Atlantic there are no gas stations, you know?"

I go back and sit down, and resume reading.

Eventually, the constant whir of the engines puts me to sleep.

I wake up at a bit of turbulence, and find Jack staring at me with both hate and defiance. Poor famous television journalist, far away from his network staff and all those sweet perks.

I check my watch.

Almost time.

I undo my seat belt one more time and go over to Jack, book in hand. "Ask you a question?" I yell.

He nods, his lips pursed in fury.

I show him the book. "Is it true you banged two Hollywood actresses at once after the Golden Globes?"

He turns away, face red.

I go back and prepare for our landing.

# CHAPTER 33

**UP FRONT, I** open the duffel bag again and strip off my civilian clothes, shivering in the cold air of the aircraft. From the open bag I take out lots of gear and carefully get dressed in what's known as "battle rattle": camouflaged BDUs, heavy boots, knee and elbow pads, body armor, helmet, MOLLE vest with a knife, night vision goggles, night vision binoculars, a flashlight, a compass, a small water bottle, a battlepack, emergency rations, a sat phone, and some new electronic doo-dads that I check out and install on my body armor.

Last and certainly not least is a modified Heckler & Koch HK416 rifle with a 10-inch barrel and two spare magazines. I take that out and I stuff my civvie clothes and shoes in the duffel bag and zip it up.

Putting the outfit on stirs up lots of memories, the most recent being the last time I had worn this gear, months ago, on my last op in Serbia, the one Allison has asked me about.

I stare at a spot in the fuselage and think of my dead teammates on that betrayed mission—Sher, Garcia, Clayton, Borozan—especially Emily Borozan. She was supposed to survive that mission and come spend long weekends at my new home at a lake in New Hampshire.

Old thoughts.

I push them away, and sit down on the webbing, checking my watch. Not long now.

Jack is really staring at me now, and he starts to yell something. I shake my head and put a finger to my lips in a "shush" motion. The C-130 makes a banking turn, there's a change in engine pitch, and I know we're on our approach.

Not long now.

There's just the slightest thump and squeal of the brakes, and the engine pitch changes again as the pilot uses reverse thrust to slow us down. I wish I could go forward and congratulate the pilot and crew, for this is one hell of a smooth landing, especially since we aren't on an airstrip.

There's a jostle as the C-130 slows even more. Then red lights brighten in the interior of the fuselage, as the ramp lowers, even as we're moving. Cold, sharp air floods in and I get up. With my knife, I cut Jack Zach free from his zip ties. His legs are wobbly but I help him up, and then we go down the inclined ramp. He collapses on the ground as the two of us step off.

Keeping my bearings, I lift him up as the C-130 continues moving away.

The red lights inside go off, and the ramp starts going back up. Then there's the roar of the engines as the black C-130 races across the desert floor and climbs into the sky. When I look carefully, I can make out a black shape, temporarily blocking out the very bright stars, but otherwise, you couldn't tell it was up there.

Jack is next to me, trembling.

All around is flat desert, distant hills and mountains, and thousands of very bright stars overhead.

We are so very alone.

# CHAPTER 34

**WITH THE C-130** gone, I get to work. From my battlepack I take out a half-dozen plastic glow sticks, snap them to light them, and toss them around on the desert floor. We're lit up in ghostly yellow-green light, and that's when Jack tries to make a run for it. I catch up with him in about five steps, drop him to the ground, and then re-secure him with plastic zip ties about the ankles and wrists.

"Pretty pathetic," I say. "Lucky for you, none of your fans are around to see you embarrass yourself."

Jack manages to get himself in a sitting position and I'm impressed when he starts laughing. "All right, all right," he says. "You've made your point."

I take some more gear out of the battlepack: a long metal piton with a hole at one end, a six-foot length of chain, and a hammer.

"What point is that, Jack?" I ask, as I start hammering the piton into the ground. It's hard going, but that's all right. It means that Jack won't be tugging this piton free anytime this week.

"That I'm a bad guy, okay? I'll admit that. But you . . . what do you think you're doing?"

I keep on pounding with the hammer. "Justice. What has to be done."

Another laugh. "Justice? In this world? Look . . . you're in a world of trouble, friend. There were witnesses at Jean-Paul who saw you kidnap me, there's the driver who helped you cross me over a state line . . . You and your military friends, you made your point. Let's not let things get out of hand."

I finish with the hammer, tug at the piton. Yep, not moving.

"Agreed," I say. "Let's not let things get out of hand."

He says, "Okay, then. Here's what I suggest, friend. Let's be best buds. Make a call, set up a flight to come pick us up, and I'll forget what you did to me. I'll buy you the best meal on the planet when we get back to Manhattan and I'll even hire you as a consultant for my network. You'll be in line to make tons of money. Just . . . call your friends back."

I lock one end of the chain to the piton. "Those aren't my friends up there, Jack, and you're not my friend, either."

"Okay, okay, like I said, point made," Jack says. "Good job on your part. I'm a bad guy. So what? There are lots of bad guys out there. What difference does one more make?"

I run the length of chain out to Jack, who unsuccessfully tries to scramble away. "Sure," I say. "There are lots of bad guys out there. But you've got a special place, all on your own. You set up American soldiers to get killed . . . for a story. You're an American. How could you do that?

Jack laughs again, even though I'm binding the chain around his ankles. "Haven't you gotten the news, friend? Nations are old fashioned. Boundaries are being erased, left and right. I'm a citizen of the world, and I've gone further than those stale constructs of the past, beyond the point of being a pawn or subject of some nation-state. I'm a multinational corporate employee, through and through. The story was there and I took it, for myself. Sorry."

I give the chain a good tug. Nothing's moving. Good. "You don't sound so sorry."

I think I've pushed him too far, because he starts swearing and calling me names and issuing threats and talking about legal action and how I'll be a broken man when this is all finished.

I let him yap without interrupting him, being the considerate fellow I am.

He stops, takes a breath. "Enough of the fooling around, asshole. Get me out of here, let me go, or my network, my lawyers, and I, personally, will destroy you."

I put the hammer away in my battlepack, pick it up, put it over my shoulder.

There.

Lights on the horizon, right on time.

Jack sees where I'm looking and his brash and demanding attitude is now gone.

"What's that?" Jack asks.

"Looks like your fellow citizens of the world are coming over to say hi."

"What do you mean?"

I adjust my gear one more time, stare straight at him so there's no confusion.

"We're in the Taliban-controlled Helmand province in Afghanistan, site of your last journalistic triumph," I say. "Have fun."

# CHAPTER 35

**JACK STARTS TO** panic, his feet pulling at the chain. "What do you mean?"

"Those trucks coming toward you belong to the Taliban," I say. "They'll be here in a few minutes, and I hear that they don't like you."

He's really tugging hard now, the chain clinking. "Oh my God . . ."

"Not sure if God's here at this moment, but I guarantee the Taliban will be, before you know it."

The clinking noise is louder. "No . . . you can't do this . . ."

I step closer to him and his struggles. I say, "Hate to say this to an up-to-date newsman like yourself, but did you see that story from this very same province three months ago? Seems there was a gathering of some Taliban leaders and while they had their hot tea and flatbread, they got three Hellfire missiles dropped in their laps."

Jack's moaning now, with his hands around the chain, pulling and pulling.

"Word is," I go on, "one of those leaders was with the Taliban unit that you were embedded with. Naturally, even though you had a hand in the slaughtering and wounding of some Americans, the Taliban think you're a spy. Suspicious boys, the Taliban. Even though you helped them with the convoy ambush, they think that was part of your cover. Pretty harsh cover, but an effective one."

"That's not true!" Jack yells.

I look out at the bright lights approaching. "Oh, I'm sure they'll listen to you, Jack, if they don't take your head off first. But then again, the Taliban aren't much in the way of beheading. They like to take their time before killing you."

Jack stops pulling at the chain, looks up to me. There are tears running down his cheeks and into his Papa Hemingway beard.

I remove the sat phone from my belt and hold it up. "I suppose I could contact the nearest Army FOB, but do you think they'll push themselves to rescue the one and only Jack Zach?"

# CHAPTER 36

**JACK GOES FROM** silent, terrified crying to bawling like a baby. Not surprising, but still, kind of disturbing considering the image he's built for himself over the years.

"Please . . . don't leave me . . . please . . ."

I say, "All right, I'm a reasonable guy." I move so that I'm directly in front of him. "Go ahead, make your case, famous tough-guy journalist. You've got about six minutes to do it."

Jack makes a snorting sound with his nose. "I'm no goddamn tough-guy journalist. I'm a fake, I'm a fraud."

"What's that?" I ask.

"You heard me!" he cries out. "I only go to places that are guaranteed safe . . . and when they're not, one of my sound men, he's ex-NYPD, really a bodyguard, is ready to kill anybody who threatens me. Shit, you know those adult diapers they sell? I always wear them in the field, for when I piss myself."

I say, "Speaking of guys who work for you, what did you do to Rachel Cooper, the wife of your cameraman, Walt?"

"I . . . I . . . Please . . ."

I make a public point of checking my watch. "Time's a-wastin.'"

"I . . . forced myself on her. I . . ."

"You assaulted her, didn't you?"

His face goes dark and my stomach drops because suddenly I realize Rachel suffered something much, much worse.

I lower my voice. "It was *sexual* assault, wasn't it?"

"Yes . . . I did . . . I . . . Please, isn't this enough?"

"There's still a bit of time left," I say. "Do go on."

"Jesus, c'mon!" he says, desperately turning his head to look at the lights, now distinct as headlights as they get closer. "I'm a piece of shit, I admit it."

In the desert air, I can now hear the approaching engines. Jack says, "And the stories about myself! Not a single word of that book of mine is true. The tale about me screwing two actresses after the Golden Globes? Pure bullshit! Pure lies."

"Just to be clear, then," I say. "Your whole life, your whole image, your whole career . . . is nothing but a lie from start to finish."

He nods his head so fast he looks like a puppet whose strings have been cut. "Yes, yes, yes . . . that's exactly right."

I check my watch one more time. "You know Edgar Allan Poe?"

He swears and says, "What the hell does that mean?"

I say, "If you were to say, 'For the love of God, Montresor,' I just might let you go."

He swears at me again, and then it's time to leave. "So long, Jack," I say. "Have a nice morning tea with your fellow citizens of the world."

I check my compass and start walking, and soon Jack is yelling at me—perhaps saying that Edgar Allan Poe phrase from "The Cask of Amontillado," perhaps not—and soon his voice is drowned out by the truck engines as I slip away into the desert darkness.

# CHAPTER 37

**I HIKE FOR** about ten minutes, following my compass and GPS, and when the land rises, it gives me a good vantage point to see what's going on behind me. I use my NVG binoculars to see Jack at the piton, desperately trying to pull it free. Three pickup trucks are arranged around him in a semicircle. Men are surrounding him, as if trying to figure out what to do with him.

Jack starts screaming. I'm surprised at how high-pitched it is, and how far it carries.

The men gather around Jack.

His screaming increases.

I shift the binoculars, examine one of the trucks. Because of the way it's parked, I see it's white and covered with desert dust, but the emblem and lettering on the side of the door is easy to see and read.

It's in the shape of an arrowhead, with a tree, mountain, lake, and white buffalo in the foreground. The lettering says NATIONAL PARK SERVICE.

I lower my binoculars. "Jack, you certainly are one dumb son of a bitch. You don't know your Edgar Allan Poe, and you certainly don't know that a four-hour flight going around in a circle won't take you to Afghanistan."

I put my binoculars away, take a nice swig of lukewarm water, wash out my mouth and spit on the ground.

"Moron," I say, and continue my march.

It's dark and rough going, but I make good time. Nobody's chasing me, nobody's gunning for me, and it's nice to be out in this wild, open, and clear desert. A little voice in me whispers to keep going, to slip into the mountains and put everything away. It wants me to start over on a real retirement where no one can find me, and it does sound tempting, save for two things.

The mission isn't quite over.

And then there's Allison.

I keep hiking.


I'm about an hour away from daybreak when I check my watch, note the time, and I unhook my sat phone and make a quick call. When the brisk female voice answers, I say, "Koala Sting, ready."

The woman says, "Confirm that, Koala Sting," and she hangs up.

I stand there in the desert, a warrior facing no war, and I wonder what will happen days and weeks from now. I decide that the future will have to take care of itself.

I turn my head to the sound of an engine, moving very fast.

From all the gear and gadgetry hanging off my webbing, I remove a strobe light and set it off. This strobe works in infrared, which means that no one can see its incessant *flash-flash* save for the man or woman overhead with night vision gear.

I turn my head to protect myself from the dust and rocks that are kicked up as an all-black MH-6 Little Bird helicopter swoops down, about fifty meters away. I lower my head and trot over. In a matter of seconds, my gear is in the back and I'm in the seat next to the pilot. I buckle in and put on a headset, the pilot works the collective and stick, checks out the red-lit instruments, and we swoop up and out over the desert.

I turn my head, trying to see the pickup trucks that have met Jack Zach, but there's nothing out there.

The pilot comes on the intercom. "How was your training mission, sir?"

"Routine," I say.

# CHAPTER 38

**A DAY LATER** I'm back at the home of Ray and Marilyn Winston, sitting on the couch in the room that had been designed for a nursery. The television is on—though muted—and Marilyn is in the kitchen, making us coffee. Allison is sitting next to me, making her dull government clothes look like high fashion, and I say, "And you let that precinct captain live?"

"Too many witnesses," she says, frowning.

"But . . . you actually complied? Really?"

I sense she's getting angrier with each passing moment and I hate to admit it, but I find it amusing. "Look, a police precinct captain came up and was giving me a ration of grief for being parked in a fire lane. He told me to move, and I told him I couldn't. It must have been the first day of his promotion and he was looking to flex his muscle. He refused to check my credentials, call anyone. Finally, he said, 'I don't care who you are. You're under arrest and your car's impounded.' I could have taken him out in about three seconds but that would have led to a lot of paperwork. Luckily, the NYPD tow truck hadn't arrived to impound the car when you dragged Jack out of there."

I don't quite know what to say, but I'm enjoying this. I'm also enjoying the bright sunny day in this house, a scent of cinnamon and the slight smell of something else I can't quite put my finger on.

"So when I was leaving the restaurant, dragging Jack Zach next to me, you were being interrogated and fingerprinted at the local precinct? Boy, I'd pay a month's pension to get prints of those photos."

She snaps back. "They don't exist. And it's your damn fault. It took you too long to get the job done."

"So says you."

"And I'm right."

Marilyn comes in, holding two mugs of coffee, and I take one and take a sip, tasting harsh bitterness, and without a word, I trade it with Allison. Marilyn smiles. "You two fighting again?"

"Like cats and dogs," Allison says.

"Like star-crossed lovers," I say, and Marilyn's smile gets wider while Allison stomps on my foot.

That's a good excuse to get up, which is what I do. I give up my place on the couch to Marilyn, and Allison says, "Hold on, we're coming up to the top of the hour," and she picks up a remote and unmutes the television.

It's a competing cable news network from INN—Jack Zach's network—and their top story is *Famed Journalist's Desert Ordeal*.

There's a male and female duo on the screen who crack jokes at each other and comment on the morning news. This time, though, they remain silent as the news package is broadcasted.

And whaddaya know, it's Jack Zach, in the desert, crying and sniffling and confessing all of his sins. And said sins were very well recorded by some of the new gear I was carrying.

Thank God I figured out how to make it work.

When the news package is completed, there's a moment of silence in the competing network's newsroom, and the woman picks up some of her script, shuffles it around, and says, "Well. That's a story."

"Sure is," her male counterpart says, peering down at something on his immaculate desk. "According to this latest news report, Jack Zach reported that he was, ah … kidnapped from Jean-Paul in Manhattan—"

"At least he had a nice final meal!" she interrupts, and her partner laughs and goes on. "Right. Kidnapped. To an isolated airstrip in New Jersey, and … forced on a black airplane, and taken to the Mojave Desert."

"A black airplane?" she says, smiling with perfect white teeth. "I thought black *helicopters* did deeds like this."

"Me, too," he says, now laughing. "And I thought they always ended up in Area 51. You know, where they can get probes stuck up their butt."

Both of them are convulsed in laughter.

Allison switches off the television.

Marilyn sits quietly, arms crossed, and says, "I told you I wanted that man destroyed. Why is he still breathing and alive?"

I say, "You asked us to hurt him, to destroy him, to make him gone, and that's what we did."

Allison says, "His network has fired him. He's a laughingstock. He'll never work in television or print or write for a website, ever again. And New York state attorney Ester Clark is looking at what he did to Rachel Cooper in New Rochelle. We got his confession to sexual assault. Ester will make sure that man goes straight to jail and that he'll be marked as a sexual predator for the rest of his life. All the while, we'll stay out of the slammer and be here for Ray instead."

"Not to mention," I say. "Do you know what they do to guys like Jack Zach in the can?"

Marilyn slowly nods—in acceptance, I hope—and a loud voice comes from the other room, "Hey! Anybody out there gonna check me out?"

The three of us get up and Ray Winston is sitting up, smiling. His complexion looks better, and his open eye is bright and shiny. Marilyn goes over, hugs him, and kisses his cheek, and I'm surprised and choked up when Allison kisses his other cheek.

I go up to him and he holds his hand out, and I give him a squeeze and he squeezes right back. "Good to see you, Top," he says, his voice firm.

"Very good to see you, too, Ray. Looks like you're finally bouncing back."

"Word is, if I keep my head straight for the next few weeks, I'll start the job of being fitted out with new legs and a new arm." He looks to Marilyn with sheer, open love. "Lord knows, I don't want my wife to get used to having a guy named Stumpy getting in the way around her house."

"Our house, fool," she says, kissing him again. He looks at me and says, "You watch, Top. A year or so from now, when I'm movin' again, I'll be just like that boy Alexander the Great, huntin' around for warmth and fun."

Marilyn says, "Don't you go huntin' without me, Raynie, or I'll hurt you."

That makes Ray laugh, and we join in. The four of us laugh and talk some more in that room. And that's when I know what the scent is, the other one I couldn't quite figure out earlier.

It's the scent of hope.

# CHAPTER 39

**OUTSIDE IN THE** strong Georgia sun, something must have gotten into our eyes, for both Allison and I are wiping at them. We go to our rental car and Allison stops, so I stop with her.

She looks back at the house and says, "You know how some people believe revenge is a waste of time, and that one should live and let live."

"Yes," I say.

"They're wrong."

"No argument from me."

Allison turns, takes the car key out, waits again, this time looking at me. "Ask you a question?"

"Ask away."

"My friend Emily. Did she die . . . bravely?"

"None braver," I say, "save for two other women I've met."

I gesture to the house. "The one in there, for fighting for her husband. And you . . . for fighting for them both."

Allison says, "I was just doing what's right."

"Aren't we all."

She seems to think about that, and says, "About doing what's right . . . Did you do anything once you got back to the States, after Serbia?"

"I squared things away."

"How?"

I say, "Remember a few months ago, there was that death of Henry Hunley, Deputy Director for Directorate Operations at the CIA?"

"Sure," she says. "The guy died of a heart attack."

"Not really," I say, knowing this woman has already seen me violate about a half dozen laws. What's one more? "He died of lead poisoning."

A smile comes over Allison's face as she finally unlocks the door.

"That's my boy, my teammate."

# CHAPTER 40

**BUT WE DON'T** go to the airport, since Allison declares the rest of our time in Georgia as a mental health day. I don't argue. She finds us a nice bed-and-breakfast outside of Atlanta, and we have a filling meal of chicken, mashed potatoes, green beans, gravy, and homemade biscuits.

When dinner is through, I escort her up the stairs and I say, "What now?"

"Tomorrow I head back to DC. I imagine you want to get back to your frozen paradise up there in New Hampshire."

"If I'm welcomed back."

She says, "Oh, you might not be welcomed back, but I bet your neighbors will give you a wide berth in the future."

"That was always the plan."

As I did in Manhattan, I go into Allison's room to make sure everything is safe and secure. The room is decorated with lots of throw pillows, vintage wallpaper, and hand soaps in the bathroom.

As before, Allison sits on the edge of her bed, jacket off, resting back on her hands, and looking up at me.

I go to the door.

Put my hand on the knob.

Then I make sure it's locked.

I walk back to her and I say, "I'm sorry . . . I'm sorry I couldn't save Emily."

She nods. "I don't need the details. I just need to know you did your best."

"I did. But it wasn't good enough."

"Sometimes that happens."

I wait now, my heart pounding, mouth dry, feeling a bit out of place. It was like the time I was about to parachute out of an aircraft into the abyss for the first time, when I knew I'd have to jump blindly and trust everything would go all right.

I lower my head, kiss her sweetly on her lips, and she responds, gripping my head with her two hands. We kiss, and we kiss, and we kiss.

I pull away, smiling at my deadly yet sweet Allison. I start to unbutton her blouse, and she whispers, "Stop."

I'm confused. "Why?"

She laughs, a sound that reaches in and charms me. "We're a team now, aren't we?" and she starts unbuttoning her blouse as well. A race quickly ensues, over who can unbutton the blouse faster, and I don't know who wins. And as I sweep her up and lie her down on the soft bed, I don't think it matters one bit.

# SOMEONE ATTACKED THE THANKSGIVING DAY PARADE. THE HUNT IS ON...

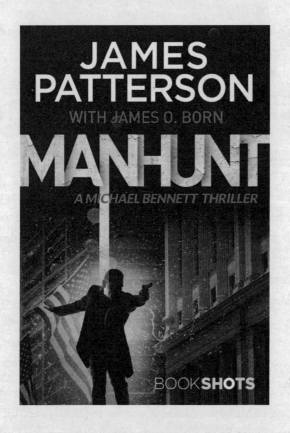

# FOR AN EXCERPT, READ ON.

**IT WAS A** bright, cloudless day and Mary Catherine had bundled the kids up like we lived at the North Pole. It was cold, with a decent breeze, but not what most New Yorkers would consider brutal. My grandfather, Seamus, would call it "crisp." It was too crisp for the old priest. He was snuggled comfortably in his quarters at Holy Name.

I wore an insulated Giants windbreaker and jeans. I admit, I looked at the kids occasionally and wished Mary Catherine had dressed me as well, but it wasn't that bad.

I herded the whole group to our usual spot, across from Rockefeller Center at 49th Street and Sixth Avenue. It was a good spot, where we could see all the floats and make our escape afterward with relatively little hassle.

I was afraid this might be the year that some of the older kids decided they'd rather sleep in than get up before dawn to make our way to Midtown. Maybe it was due to Chrissy's tearful conversation with Brian, but everyone was up and appeared excited despite the early hour.

Now we had staked out our spot for the parade, and were

waiting for the floats. It was perfect outside and I gave in to the overwhelming urge to lean over and kiss Mary Catherine.

Chrissy and Shawna crouched in close to us as Jane flirted with a couple of boys from Nebraska—after I'd spoken to them, of course. They were nice young men, in their first year at UN Kearney.

We could tell by the reaction of the crowd that the parade was coming our way. We sat through the first couple of marching bands and earthbound floats before we saw one of the stars of the parade: Snoopy, in his red scarf, ready for the Red Baron.

Of course, Eddie had the facts on the real Red Baron. He said, "You know, he was an ace in World War I for Germany. His name was Manfred von Richthofen. He had over eighty kills in dogfights."

The kids tended to tune out some of Eddie's trivia, but Mary Catherine and I showed interest in what he said. It was important to keep a brain like that fully engaged.

Like any NYPD officer, on or off duty, I keep my eyes open and always know where the nearest uniformed patrol officer is. Today I noticed a tall, young African American officer trying to politely corral people in our area, who ignored him and crept onto the street for a better photo.

I smiled, knowing how hard it is to get people to follow any kind of rules unless there is an immediate threat of arrest.

Then I heard it.

At first, I thought it was a garbage truck banging a dumpster as it emptied it. Then an engine revved down 49th Street, and I turned to look.

I barely had any time to react. A white Ford step-van truck barreled down the street directly toward us. It was gaining speed, though it must have had to slow down to get by the dump truck parked at the intersection of 49th and Sixth as a blockade.

Shawna was ten feet to my right, focused on Snoopy. She was directly in the path of the truck.

It was like I'd been shocked with electricity. I jumped from my spot and scooped up Shawna a split second before the truck rolled past us. I heard Mary Catherine shriek as I tumbled, with Shawna, on the far side of the truck.

The truck slammed into spectators just in front of us. One of the boys from Nebraska bounced off the hood with a sickening thud. He lay in a twisted heap on the rough asphalt. His University of Nebraska jacket was sprayed with a darker shade of red as blood poured from his mouth and ears.

The truck rolled onto the parade route until it collided with a sponsor vehicle splattered with a Kellogg's logo. The impact sent a young woman in a purple pageant dress flying from the car and under the wheels of a float.

Screams started to rise around me, but I couldn't take my eyes off the truck.

The driver made an agile exit from the crumpled driver's door and stood right next to the truck. Over his face, he wore a red scarf with white starburst designs.

He shouted, *"Hawqala!"*

**I STOOD IN** shock like just about everyone else near me. This was not something we were used to seeing on US soil.

Eddie and Jane, crouching on the sidewalk next to me, both stood and started to move away from me.

I grabbed Eddie's wrist.

He looked back at me and said, "We've got to help them."

Jane had paused right next to him as I said, "We don't know what's going to happen."

As I said it, the driver of the truck reached in his front jacket pocket and pulled something out. I couldn't identify it exactly, but I knew it was a detonator.

I shouted as loud as I could, "Everyone down!" My family knew to lie flat on the sidewalk and cover their faces with their hands. A few people in the crowd listened to me as well. Most were still in shock or sobbing.

The driver hit the button on the detonator and immediately there was a blinding flash, and what sounded like a thunderclap echoed among all the buildings.

I couldn't turn away as I watched from the pavement. The

blast blew the roof of the truck straight into the air almost thirty feet. I felt it in my guts. A fireball rose from the truck.

The driver was dazed and stumbled away from the truck as the roof landed on the asphalt not far from him.

Now there was absolute pandemonium. It felt like every person on 49th Street was screaming. The blast had rocked the whole block.

The parade was coming to an abrupt stop. Parade vehicles bumped one another and the marching band behind the step van scattered. A teenager with a trumpet darted past me, looking for safety.

The driver pushed past spectators on the sidewalk near us and started to run back down 49th Street where he had driven the truck.

The ball of flame was still rising like one of the floats. Then I noticed a couple of the floats were rising in the air as well. The human anchors had followed instinct and run for their lives.

Snoopy was seventy-five feet in the air now.

Several Christmas tree ornaments as big as Volkswagens, with only three ropes apiece, made a colorful design as they passed the middle stories of Rockefeller Center.

I glanced around, but didn't see any uniformed cops close. The one young patrolman I had seen keeping people in place was frantically trying to help a child who had been struck by the truck.

I had no radio to call for backup. I just had my badge and my off-duty pistol hidden in my waistband.

There had been plenty of cops early, but now I saw that some of them had been hurt in the explosion, others were trying to help victims. It was mayhem, and no one was chasing the perp. I was it. I had to do something.

# ALSO BY JAMES PATTERSON

## ALEX CROSS NOVELS

Along Came a Spider
Kiss the Girls
Jack and Jill
Cat and Mouse
Pop Goes the Weasel
Roses are Red
Violets are Blue
Four Blind Mice
The Big Bad Wolf
London Bridges
Mary, Mary
Cross
Double Cross
Cross Country
Alex Cross's Trial (*with Richard DiLallo*)
I, Alex Cross
Cross Fire
Kill Alex Cross
Merry Christmas, Alex Cross
Alex Cross, Run
Cross My Heart
Hope to Die
Cross Justice
Cross the Line
The People vs. Alex Cross

## THE WOMEN'S MURDER CLUB SERIES

1st to Die
2nd Chance (*with Andrew Gross*)
3rd Degree (*with Andrew Gross*)
4th of July (*with Maxine Paetro*)
The 5th Horseman (*with Maxine Paetro*)
The 6th Target (*with Maxine Paetro*)

7th Heaven (*with Maxine Paetro*)
8th Confession (*with Maxine Paetro*)
9th Judgement (*with Maxine Paetro*)
10th Anniversary (*with Maxine Paetro*)
11th Hour (*with Maxine Paetro*)
12th of Never (*with Maxine Paetro*)
Unlucky 13 (*with Maxine Paetro*)
14th Deadly Sin (*with Maxine Paetro*)
15th Affair (*with Maxine Paetro*)
16th Seduction (*with Maxine Paetro*)

## DETECTIVE MICHAEL BENNETT SERIES

Step on a Crack (*with Michael Ledwidge*)
Run for Your Life (*with Michael Ledwidge*)
Worst Case (*with Michael Ledwidge*)
Tick Tock (*with Michael Ledwidge*)
I, Michael Bennett (*with Michael Ledwidge*)
Gone (*with Michael Ledwidge*)
Burn (*with Michael Ledwidge*)
Alert (*with Michael Ledwidge*)
Bullseye (*with Michael Ledwidge*)
Haunted (*with James O. Born*)

## PRIVATE NOVELS

Private (*with Maxine Paetro*)
Private London (*with Mark Pearson*)
Private Games (*with Mark Sullivan*)
Private: No. 1 Suspect (*with Maxine Paetro*)
Private Berlin (*with Mark Sullivan*)
Private Down Under (*with Michael White*)

Private L.A. (*with Mark Sullivan*)
Private India (*with Ashwin Sanghi*)
Private Vegas (*with Maxine Paetro*)
Private Sydney (*with Kathryn Fox*)
Private Paris (*with Mark Sullivan*)
The Games (*with Mark Sullivan*)
Private Delhi (*with Ashwin Sanghi*)

### NYPD RED SERIES

NYPD Red (*with Marshall Karp*)
NYPD Red 2 (*with Marshall Karp*)
NYPD Red 3 (*with Marshall Karp*)
NYPD Red 4 (*with Marshall Karp*)

### DETECTIVE HARRIET BLUE SERIES

Never Never (*with Candice Fox*)
Fifty Fifty (*with Candice Fox*)

### STAND-ALONE THRILLERS

The Thomas Berryman Number
Sail (*with Howard Roughan*)
Swimsuit (*with Maxine Paetro*)
Don't Blink (*with Howard Roughan*)
Postcard Killers (*with Liza Marklund*)
Toys (*with Neil McMahon*)
Now You See Her (*with Michael Ledwidge*)
Kill Me If You Can (*with Marshall Karp*)
Guilty Wives (*with David Ellis*)
Zoo (*with Michael Ledwidge*)
Second Honeymoon (*with Howard Roughan*)
Mistress (*with David Ellis*)
Invisible (*with David Ellis*)
Truth or Die (*with Howard Roughan*)
Murder House (*with David Ellis*)

Woman of God (*with Maxine Paetro*)
Hide and Seek
Humans, Bow Down (*with Emily Raymond*)
The Black Book (*with David Ellis*)
Murder Games (*with Howard Roughan*)
Black Market
The Moores are Missing (*with Loren D. Estleman, Sam Hawken and Ed Chatterton*)
The Midnight Club
The Store (*with Richard DiLallo*)
The Family Lawyer (*with Robert Rotstein, Christopher Charles and Rachel Howzell Hall*)

### BOOKSHOTS

Black & Blue (*with Candice Fox*)
Cross Kill
Private Royals (*with Rees Jones*)
The Trial (*with Maxine Paetro*)
Chase (*with Michael Ledwidge*)
Hidden (*with James O. Born*)
Malicious (*with James O. Born*)
The Exile (*with Alison Joseph*)
The Shut-In (*with Duane Swierczynski*)
Private Gold (*with Jassy Mackenzie*)
Detective Cross
Deadly Cargo (*with Will Jordan*)
The Women's War (*with Shan Serafin*)
The Medical Examiner (*with Maxine Paetro*)
The Dolls (*with Kecia Bal*)
Absolute Zero (*with Ed Chatterton*)
The End (*with Brendan DuBois*)
Manhunt (*with James O. Born*)